Nouran Daoud is a young aspiring author from Egypt. She has always had a passion for writing and plans on writing many more books in the future. When she is not spending her free time writing, she always enjoys doing many different activities such as skating, swimming and more. *One Last Find* is her debut novel and she had so much fun through the whole process. She can't wait to release more books in the future.

Nouran Daoud

ONE LAST FIND

AUSTIN MACAULEY PUBLISHERS®

LONDON ∗ CAMBRIDGE ∗ NEW YORK ∗ SHARJAH

ISBN – 9789948742968 – (Paperback)
ISBN – 9789948742975 – (E-Book)

Application Number: MC-10-01-8331915
Age Classification: 17+

The age group that matches the content of the books has been classified according to the age classification system issued by the UAE Media Council.

Printer Name: iPrint Global Ltd
Printer Address: Witchford, England

First Published 2024
AUSTIN MACAULEY PUBLISHERS FZE
Sharjah Publishing City
P.O Box [519201]
Sharjah, UAE
www.austinmacauley.ae
+971 655 95 202

Thank you to everyone who has supported me throughout my journey of writing this book. Including my family and friends. I wouldn't be where I am today without them, so thank you so much!

Chapter 1
My Story

"I'll find him, just you wait!" I called after the figure of my retreating colleague. I huffed out a harsh sigh when their figure disappeared right around the corner.

I looked away from their previous spot to focus on storing my magnifying glass and torch away in my locker.

I slammed the door shut with a bang.

I was walking down the office hallways, with the nauseating stench of bleach clinging to me, and my hands itching to be washed in the office bathroom. My mind was drifting to it all.

The blood, the guts and the vomit all invade my senses.

I was jolted to reality when Marcus, my boss, had synced paces with me. We flanked each other, walking side by side until I had reached my desk.

I leaned over my desk, organizing and shuffling through the files I needed while Marcus lingered far too close for comfort.

That's when I felt Marcus's hand clamped down on my shoulder and forcibly halted against me. I blew a harsh breath through my teeth and shrugged his hand off before looking over at him.

He immediately sneered as soon as my eyes were on him. He gave me a glare you'd give to someone you hated. Someone you despised so much.

I stared at him for a second before letting out a loud sigh, making sure he could hear it. I looked away, trying to set my sights back on the papers I had been focusing on before and that's when I could feel Marcus' gaze burning holes in the back of my head.

"Well?" Marcus basically spat, breaking the silence.

I almost flinched, but kept my expression placid.

I paused, briefly looking at the missing poster in my pile before finally raising my gaze back up to meet his pinning one.

"Hey, Marcus. What exactly is it that you want from me, causing you to follow me around? I'm busy right now preparing files for tomorrow," I questioned evenly.

"Yeah that's exactly why I'm here. How about you forget about it? Don't even bother coming back tomorrow. You used to do so much better," Marcus snapped harshly, leaning in slightly with a glare.

I squirmed under his gaze and fought hard to not break eye contact.

"You can't seem to sort out your priorities anymore. Not like before, at least," Marcus said in a much looser tone, retreating a couple steps back with a smirk plastered on his face.

Though I really liked work, I had been sick of Marcus treating everyone including me like we were beneath him. Like we don't belong.

I clenched my jaw.

"All you can think about is nothing but defective meritless ideas," Marcus insisted smugly. His voice boomed and echoed sharply throughout the offices.

All I could think about was every other day, when Marcus would taunt as he snorted at us workers who lived at starvation levels.

"If you don't like how things work around here, maybe you just shouldn't be here. Maybe you guys should find new jobs, somewhere far away."

That's when I decided to take a break from work. A break that I knew deep down I deserved after all the humiliation I had been through.

I quietly started to think about the reasoning behind Marcus' behavior.

After all, I was a detective. It was quite literally my life's work to figure out people's behaviors.

I felt like Marcus was a two-faced person who didn't care about helping others.

Yet, how could he be in this line of work? The main focus was to find out who the bad guys were.

There was so much more emotionality to being a great detective than I had ever expected.

I wonder how Marcus was able to go through with it all when in reality, he has nothing more than a cold, dead heart.

In every case we have worked on, there were so many heartbreaking stories on all sides and it was up to us to find out who was guilty and who wasn't.

Day in and day out, I quickly realized that the world of being a detective was far from the glamorized world I had seen in the media.

Every single day, we had to show up for people on their worst possible days.

We had to confront the darkest aspects of humanity. The crimes that shatter and ruin so many different lives, people's motives that had caused them to commit the worst acts possible.

It makes you want to quit.

But if we all quit, who is going to help people?

A haunting solitude often hangs on my shoulders being a daily reminder that getting justice for families can be lonely.

It is our job to help people but sometimes I wonder, who is going to help us?

Each one of us detectives carries a pocketful of stories that never fade away.

The toll can be so immense at us that some of us grapple and fight everyday with the thoughts of suicide. The horrors we witness everyday ruin us more and more.

They ruin us psychologically because protecting society while being exposed to some of the darkest crimes is a burden some of us cannot handle.

The more cases that I get, the greater the barrier gets between me and the outside world.

I have to constantly remind myself that not everyone is out to get me.

Seeing people get murdered everyday makes you start believing that everyone else is tainted by darkness. It seeps into your perception and twists every little thing someone does to make you start questioning them.

I hated how it made me feel.

I hated the feeling so much.

The pressure to solve cases, having to see the raw pain of victims and their families.

It makes you constantly remember your family and all you want to do is call them.

Check up on them.

Make sure they're safe.

As I stood inside of my workplace, with a box of my belongings in my hand, I softly placed them down on the hardwood floor.

I quickly slid my phone out from my jacket pocket, while jumbling through a bunch of items, and struck the call button with my thumb.

"Hey, what's up?" I greeted warmly.

"Heyy! Just getting ready to go to my yoga class," Isabella, my wife, softly mumbled as I heard her car keys jingling in the background.

"Okay, I know this isn't a good time but I just got suspended from my job. It's nothing serious, but I'll tell you more information later," I quietly uttered, after picking up the courage to reveal this to her.

I quickly hung up before we could finish our conversation.

I couldn't bear hearing her reaction because the last thing I would ever want to do was to disappoint her. She had always supported me no matter what it was that I had wanted to do.

Isabella had known how my job had taken a toll on my mental health, but she didn't know how bad it had gotten.

She had constantly tried to remind me that while there is darkness in the world, not everyone is defined by it.

She did help me, temporarily.

Her reminders were essential for me to maintain my grasp on reality.

That's when I decided to write this book for those who are skeptical of everything.

Those who shiver as they walk down eerie, gloomy streets with dead leaves crunching under their feet and their minds wandering around all kinds of thoughts surrounding murder cases that happened all those years ago.

It's for those who are cautious around everyone, whether they are close people or strangers, those who ensure they know each person before putting their trust in them.

Don't beat yourself up about it. One fact is that you can't know something for sure until you truly know it. We all learn from our mistakes, even those who seem to do everything so promptly and without hesitation: they too often forget even the littlest of things.

Do the best that you can with the knowledge you have now.

It's brutal not knowing whether you are right or not, whether you have chosen the right path or not, whether you deserve something or not based on what you've done. It's exhausting, mentally and physically.

As I continued packing and throwing piles of useless items I had trashed in my office, I started getting ready to leave a job I had loved so much.

A job I had spent years studying and practicing for.
A job that was so dear to me. I couldn't help but notice my flickering phone screen with vibrations of notifications piling on.

All of them were missed calls from my wife.

Though she had the right to know, it was up to me whether I wanted to tell her everything about why I was suspended from my job. Whether that was today, another day, or perhaps even never. I never was the type to share a lot with people, not even with my own wife.

I hadn't known Isabella very long before I proposed to her, we had only been together for a couple of months.

Sometimes, I feel like the only reason she agreed to marry me was because she felt bad for me. But I wouldn't know.

She truly is the sweetest person I have ever come across.

That may be the reason I had gotten so attached to her and proposed so quickly.

Once I was finished packing everything I had once thought of as the career I would be practicing for the rest of my life, boxes upon boxes of solved cases I had worked on, photographs of people I had met along the way, I noticed a bottle in the distance.

It was at the very back of my desk and I didn't recognize it straight away. However, as I picked it up, I quickly remembered what this was.

The bottle read:

"Sertraline."

An antidepressant I had started taking when I first started the job.

It helped relieve the mental pain I felt, temporarily.

However, that was before all the side effects started acting up.

I slid it down my pocket, even though deep down I knew that it was probably best to get rid of it.

I hesitantly picked up my phone and answered one of my wife's phone calls.

Isabella mumbles at me as I could hear her emotions falling through the abyss with only her sadness being visible.

"What happened? What happened at your job? What happened to you? *What happened to us?* I don't understand what went wrong."

Deep down, I knew when everything had started going wrong.

Though I was embarrassed, I knew it was wrong of me to keep leading Isabella on. It was wrong to make her deal with all this and make her believe it was okay.

Make her believe that it was normal.

She deserved a better life. She didn't deserve to be one of those people who sat by the window, day after day, with her gaze fixed on the world outside.

Did she feel as trapped at home just as I felt at work?

Did she hate me?

She didn't deserve to be one of those people whose eyes were fixed on the minutes ticking away slowly like a fading heartbeat, waiting for me to come home from work.

That is if I had come home from work that day.

I sometimes sit at work, wondering if Isabella would look at her ring and ponder on if she thought the promise I made to her when I gave it to her was being tested by my constant absence.

I loved her so much.

I loved her more than I loved myself.

Yet I knew that if I really loved her, I wouldn't do this to her.

I didn't want each passing car's headlights outside of our home window to catch her attention because she thought it was me coming home.

When I finally seemed to gain the courage to talk, I came to the realization that I actually had nothing to say.

There was nothing I wanted to discuss with her. I stood still, waiting for her to give me any kind of response, any kind of signal.

The silence she had was louder than a speaker on full volume. That silence was a silence filled with sorrow.

It was a silence that proved how fragile we humans are, yet it was more comforting than anything I had ever heard because it was her silence.

Isabella had many qualities, yet I believe her being with me meant she had to give some up. I didn't want that for her.

Deep down, I had always hoped she would eventually get tired of me. That she would eventually just leave.

Yet, through the labyrinth of my daily mental struggles, she constantly stood by my side, devoted to helping me feel better.

Why did she have to love me?

Why did she have to meet me?

Her commitment to me showed that love could wither away the storms of the mind and offer a glimmer of peace even if it's only for a couple of minutes a day.

Her patience shone the brightest during my darkest hours, yet I couldn't help but wonder:

Why did she love me?

I had nothing good to offer her.

Only my mood that would constantly ebb and flow unpredictably.

Only the fragile veneer mask that I wore every day to shield others from my rage.

So, why did she love me?

I could hear Isabella's sniffles before she finally gained the courage to speak, "Noah, I don't think I can do this anymore. I thought what you were going through was going to be over soon enough. I thought you were just stressed from work. I thought that all the secrecy you've been going through was going to be over soon. I was wrong about you. I was wrong about all of it."

Hearing that made my heart heavy. I started to feel dizzy as the tears that had built up in my eyes were blurring my vision.

I had watched her dreams wither away while being with her, and it was all my fault. She had so much unfulfilled potential, and her being with me meant she had to give it all up.

"I'm sorry—," I managed to mutter out. Yet I realized it was too late to continue expressing the rest. She had hung up the phone before I could finish.

In the aftermath of her leaving me, waves of queasiness rolled through my stomach and the world around me seemed to tilt and blur, mirroring the disarray within my heart.

My stomach churned with a mixture of grief, shock, disbelief and the weight of her absence hitting me with a force that only seemed to consume me.

The more I thought about it, the more I heard a bittersweet echo running through my mind.

It felt like there was a dagger twisting inside of my chest. I could feel the already small room I was in closing in around me and my trembling hands now in rhythm with my heartbeat.

I stood still, waiting for this feeling to go away.

I let out a sigh before looking out of the window of a place I would be banished from soon. The once-bright sunshine was overtaken by silver storms gathering and quenching at the earth.

All the clouds in the sky were now nothing but thick, dark fogs hovering over the skies, bringing misery over the town. I stood there, watching them before I was shocked back to reality.

"Are you leaving anytime soon? Listen, I know you're obsessed with this place, but I have actual work to attend to so if you don't mind, leave soon. We don't have all day to wait for you," Marcus stated.

I glanced over at him, meeting his harsh gaze from where he stood by the office's doorway.

I took a deep breath, trying to hold as much air in since it only felt like it was escaping away from me.

"Marcus, why do you think you have the right to treat us all like we're beneath you? Every single person working here will leave and when you're left all alone, don't come crying to everyone, telling them to come back to you," I spat back at Marcus.

Consumed by all the uncontrollable rage that had built up inside of me, I felt like a tempest.

The world around me blurred as anger consumed my senses and all I could see was Marcus' faded figure staring directly at me.

The impulse that I was feeling to destroy everything around me was an uncontrollable urge.

I stormed towards any items that I could see in the room and before I knew it, I found myself unleashing all the fury I had felt on the items around me.

Soon, the floor was filled with shattered glass, splintered wood and ripped up pieces of paper scattered all around.

The storm of anger I had gradually built up, had formed into a huge ball of rage and the rush of adrenaline that fueled my fury started to go away, slowly being replaced with a sense of peace. My thoughts started to untangle and I had seen what my actions had resulted in.

The aftermath of my outburst was the fragments of broken objects that had mirrored how I had felt during that time.

Breathing deeply, I didn't know what to do.

What had I just done?

Looking around the room, a wave of discomfort washed over me as a sudden hush fell over my coworkers.

I could feel the heavy weight of every pair of gazed eyes in the room fixed upon me and the sensation was unnerving.

My heart started to race and a prickling feeling of discomfort crept over my skin, making me feel like the odd one out in the room. I could feel Marcus' judgmental look as he looked around the room and his laughter seemed to flow seamlessly.

I felt like an intruder in this social tapestry.

I slam shoulders with Marcus as I rush to make my way out of the room, leaving him stunned.

I felt so vulnerable and exposed and my movements became hesitant. I almost felt like every step I took would lead to me doing something that would trigger my anger once more.

Yet for some odd reason, every step I took away from my work place, a sense of relief strangely washed over me, and it felt like a weight had been lifted off my shoulders.

I decided to call my best friend, someone I relied on for everything. His name was Liam. He was also a detective who would occasionally work on different cases with me.

He answered.

"Hey, Liam. Marcus did it again. I am so done with him. I was so angry, I don't even know what happened," I began to ramble.

"Wait what? Listen, if you need me to come and help you out with anything, let me know. You know how Marcus is, he always does this. I am honestly so used to it by now," Liam replied, clearly worried about me.

"I know. Listen, I need to go. I'll call you later though," I muttered at him before hanging up.

I now knew I wasn't going to be controlled any longer by anyone.

I felt free.

I hated Marcus with my whole heart. There wasn't anything anyone could do to stop him from playing manipulative mind games towards us all.

He's the type of person to take credit from another person and take all the fame for himself. He doesn't realize that he is the one true loser through it all.

He can take all the credit he wants. He can even fire anyone he wants, whenever he wants, but he only cheats himself of the loving bonds and support a team provides whenever they are together.

He'll toss and turn in bed, wondering why no one but him is on his side. Yet deep down, he knows everything he does in life is wrong and the best thing he did to me was let me leave the workplace we shared together.

After leaving the building, I hopped into my car. Strangely enough, I was excited for what was to come. However, I gazed down at my phone, realizing that Isabella couldn't deal with me anymore. *I was now all alone in this.*

Deep down, I knew that this was going to happen eventually. I wasn't surprised nor upset, I only felt numb, and maybe even a little *empty*. I had expected it after our conversation on the phone.

Isabella's text read,

"The past couple of years that I have known you were one of my best years in life. We spent so much time together, getting to know each other, getting to make happy memories together. Yet for some reason, I now feel like I don't know you at all. Now, all I can seem to do is flip through all the memories we made together and feel comfort inside of me knowing that you are and forever will be part of my background. These memories have kept me warm, even when storms are striking the living. We've flown to every place, and we've laughed every laugh. You'll forever be part of the tale

I tell to others, but I don't think me and you were meant to last. I'm sorry, I will forever be here if you need me."

/Split-splat/

/Split-splat/

/Split-splat/

As the rain drops dropped down from the sky, the rhythmic pattern of rain against the windshield wipers of my car matched my racing thoughts as I drove through the misty veil of emotions.

I felt like I had failed as not only being a husband to Isabella, but also being there for her.

The way each raindrop streaked down the glass windows felt like an echo of the tears I had fought so hard to hold back this whole time.

I was trying so hard to be brave, but for whom?

For what?

The only feeling that had been familiar to me for the past couple of weeks was the feeling of loneliness. I am constantly surrounded by my coworkers and have always had friends, but I felt like a lonely person.

As I kept driving around, the dampness outside didn't seem to get any better. The rain outside had caused the storm to intensify even more.

The road stretched out before me, and it was a long path that seemed to mirror my journey through the turbulence of how I felt about all of this.

I knew Isabella leaving me was for the better, but how could I fully accept it? She was the only good thing that had happened in my life in a long time and to think that she won't be in my life anymore was killing me.

I pulled over, overwhelmed by all of the emotions I was feeling.

I couldn't help but recall and think about everything we had been through, from the first day till the last day I had seen her. They say behind every cry you shed, anger is the reason for it all.

However, I think it's caused because of all your emotions at once. At that moment, I washed away my inner clutter that had been roaming around for so long by what I could only think about doing, *sobbing.*

I was so tired of everything going on around me: first being suspended from work then Isabella leaving me. I couldn't help but think about all the moments I had being a detective, how I had to study for so long, yet it was all worth it.

For us detectives, the decisions we make play an important role in what happens; whether you're going to ruin someone's life when they may not deserve it in the end.

Whether you're going to catch the real bad guy, or if you're going to sentence an innocent man to his demise in a prison cell.

The only thing I could think of doing at the moment was to grab the blank notebook I had stored in my glove box for a long time. For a while, its only purpose was to collect dust, but that was going to change starting today. I got out a pen and started scribbling everything that came to mind.

If you're reading this, you've been able to get your hands on a detective's diary. In here, you'll find many secrets no eye, that later wasn't found lifeless, has seen. Eventually left abandoned, forgotten, perhaps even feared by many generations of people to come.

It contains puzzles and mysteries of a detective trying to solve crimes and his journey along it about how deep inside his cold heart, filled with so much heroism and courage that it caused many people to have forgotten and ignored all the fright and terror within him.

I had forgotten about all the fear and horror that I had and simply banished it from existence until it was no longer there.

When people tell you something, especially over and over again, you will eventually start to believe it even if it's not the truth. You will simply believe in it and forget the actual truth, along with all the evidence backing it up. It will directly vanish from sight and mind.

Placing my notebook down, I quickly kept driving away. I didn't know where to go, whether I was making the right decision by driving away or not. All I knew was that I had to leave and get out of my car soon.

As I was driving, I realized that what we do in this life may echo on and on for eternity. Though at the same time, people will forget things straight after they've happened and won't look back at them ever again.

We arrive on this Earth and soon we leave. We leave behind many things. We leave behind all the people we had met, and all the kind souls we had helped.

Sometimes, we don't realize it until it's too late, but our lives are filled with many pleasing memories, but the best ones we remember are those where we gained something from them – whether it be big or small.

You may get a small trophy from something, yet you will always cherish it. One day, people are grieving over the death of a kind soul and the next, they have completely forgotten about them and it leads to everyone returning back to their normal life.

I can vouch as a witness for this happening over multiple occasions by many different people.

An admirable soul who helps whoever they can, whenever they can.

A nice person who lived their whole life just minding their own business; those who are and forever will be fair and not judgmental, regardless of race, gender, educational status, religion, or economic status. They are kind-hearted and treat everyone with respect, regardless of what you do for a living. It is those who treat people with care and compassion.

They are the sweetest, kindest of people, yet for some odd reason, they are not that nice to themselves.

One good person isn't another person's good person. It all depends on the perspective you have. They can be described as a wholesome person. A person who is someone's child, someone's sibling, or someone's best friend.

In this world, with so much hatred and hostility, you can easily find people who are selfish, manipulative, racist, and would treat you less than a human. In my dictionary, anyone opposite of these people is nice. They do what makes them happy without hurting anyone else.

We live in a generation like no other: a generation with technology swallowing and feeding on people's sanity.

We live in a generation where people feel the need to fill their faces up with chemicals until they can no longer breathe, in order to just feel beautiful.

A generation where people may always be drawn to each other, their story with each person was never finished, it still had a long way and journey to go. There are so many pages left that are still not read; it would be tiring to put it down and just go on with a journey so long.

Now you may be wondering, who am I? Why am I writing this?

My name is Noah Ledger and well, after a lot of thinking, I've decided to write a diary to help me get a better perspective on things and if I ever get a job again, it will help me with my cases.

I'll be able to keep track of everything and it'll get a lot easier for me. Not only that, I might even be able to work on multiple cases at once.

I might get hired by a powerful person and well, earn a lot of money from it. I've never been money greedy but this might be my only chance to earn a quick buck.

Being a detective is like opening a new eye to a world you've never seen before. A world full of lies and deception, to the point where you didn't know it was possible for it to be like that. Typically, I don't assume the worst of things but once I saw the world through a detective's eyes, I knew that it was nothing like how I thought it was.

Rather, it was even more miserable than you could ever know. Every day, I'm filled with regret knowing I chose this life for myself; a life so pathetic that people only know what I choose and allow for them to know.

They can only see what I let them see and sometimes, only let them interpret things however they like.

Whether they like to view it as a satisfying lie to please them rather than the unpleasant truth to upset them.

Opening your eyes is realizing the hard truth. It's a wake-up call and a warning to all of humanity; once you see it, there is no turning back. If you'd like to turn back to before knowing all the truth, you can't.

Corruption is a great evil of society, if not one *the* greatest evil of society. A world of fright and danger.

A world where there is no escape. There is danger on all sides, all routes, and all streets. If you tried to get away, you just couldn't. This is the harsh reality in which we live. A reality so wicked and wrong, parents will try to protect their children from it as much as they can.

Parents always declared and reassured the children, "Monsters aren't real; they aren't under your bed."

What they didn't know is that monsters are very much real. They can be found anywhere and everywhere. They roam through the streets of the Earth with eyes full of darkness and evil as they try to find their next victim.

There are so many monsters out there, each with a different backstory. You and I could be monsters, and could even be defending monsters out there.

The monsters that we see today were once looking at the world through innocent eyes, all thoughts and feelings of positivity and amazement.

They were once full of content and joy as they sang songs and were carefree of the world. They looked out to the sky as it would slowly change from the pitch-black darkness into a bright-orange sky full of sunshine. They were once little kids, little kids who were brought into this world and considered a blessing by many.

We came from darkness and therefore must return to darkness. The way I see it, humans simply live in order to live.

We live and stay ignorant of all the signs of death coming your way. From exhaustion all the way to health complications, death is and always will be there, till the end of time, infinite or finite.

Some kinds of deaths don't have a cure, at least that's what people have said and will remain to do so over the years. If you think about it, hospitals would be shut down if it weren't for ill patients; they survive and feed off from our sickness, just like any other business would.

People may say if you're lucky, you'll live a long life until your heart suddenly can't bear to beat, until your eyes suddenly can't bear to open or until your lungs suddenly can't provide you with enough oxygen in order to survive.

Not everyone thinks that, though.

It's not that simple for everyone. Some die slowly, bit by bit and death doesn't just randomly strike them. For some, they end up slowly killing themselves naturally or willingly, whether it be their desire for smoking one last smoke or them losing all aspiration and desire for their life and survival along with their self-esteem.

Yet for others, their self-worth has been slaughtered so much by others that they feel unworthy in life. Some people will kill you leisurely until you can't take it anymore. They find peace in your disturbance and annoyance, and they will simply manage to find pleasure in it.

The way I see those who insult and belittle others, similar to my old boss, Marcus, most likely feel that way about themselves and can't help but take it out on others.

It got me thinking about that one time I had met someone so special to me that I had been willing to give up everything I had worked so hard for. The things that I had spent so much time and energy working for in a temporary world.

The world we will all eventually get to see and embrace but what if we are already in the real world? No child should ever have to go through the suffering of wondering whether or not they feel safe going to school.

No parent should ever have to wonder whether or not their kids will return home that day. Unfortunately for many, the kids have left and have never returned home safely to their families.

It has left many families grieving and traumatized from actions that could have easily been stopped and prevented if people tried harder. You'll realize that each person you see on the streets has their own story, they are somebody's child.

Those people you see and meet with everyday have got people surrounding them, they have friends and perhaps lovers, but in the end, they have got someone waiting for them. They have crossed paths with people who have understood them so well that they have called them "their person".

They see parts of themselves in other people and they realize how lucky they are to have them, especially when they feel recognized around them.

However, not all people have a person. They don't have a person to go to when they are in doubt and need support.

I know that I don't have a person, perhaps that's why I like to distract myself with my work, my sleep and other things. Some people just can't bear to handle loneliness.

How do you expect people to choose you when you can't even bear to choose yourself in a room full of people?

A room full of people harshly speaking to one another, yet the loudest sound in the room is your silence. It brings so much attention to you and not the good kind.

People find silence peaceful and calming. A living heaven in front of their eyes. It's like a gentle scenery where the cold wind blows gently towards your skin and the wind rustles through the silent melody.

I don't find it soothing, since it is not the silence everyone is used to.

It's the silence of sorrow where everything is so loud yet you can't hear it at all. That is my silence.

As a detective, it has always been my job to catch any murderer I see, even if that means it's my own family.

You see, I was pretty good at it and that resulted in many people hiring me for many cases and without a doubt, I have not let *any* of them down.

Even though I have a good reputation, it hasn't always been like this. I used to cover-up for some murderers, some frauds and even myself. After I was caught doing that, I soon stopped, or at least I tried to stop.

People can't always quit actions that are referred to as their "bad habits". They are formed more easily than good habits and are almost always the hardest to stop. Question is, how do we know what truly is wrong and right? Perhaps there is no such thing and society has made up the terms, along with everything else that mankind knows about.

It's like we are put into this floating rock in the middle of nowhere and expected to follow certain ethics in order to put up with society's expectations except that is how it really is. It's our true reality.

A 6-year-old little girl, expected to not act "child-like", a 14-year-old girl, expected to not act "grown-up".

They will never be pleased or satisfied and yet, we all sit in silence and just get on with our own lives.

The life we created.

If anything, we are to blame for all the chaos caused around us.

As time passed, we evolved and grew. Millions of years ago in evolution is what we now refer to as a part of history, filled with murders and diseases.

It's what people refer to as the "bad" that happened in the past. What they don't know is that to this day, the same events happen over and over again just like they did centuries ago.

The worst part of it all is that this time, it's being hidden and covered by many to not show the disturbing parts of our world.

The sight of blood, for many, would cause them to startle; they would be questioning where it came from. For me, I had gotten so used to it that when I accidentally cut myself using a knife on my lunch and blood came streaming down my finger. I had forgotten to react.

I simply wiped it off while I had remembered a crime scene that happened more than five years ago near the dark desolate street, where even the brave wouldn't dare cross.

That side of the world was no stranger to multiple crimes over the last few years. It had gotten so bad that police had been thinking of shutting it down.

Anyone with even the greatest amount of heroism and self-preservation wouldn't be caught dead there, but in the end, buried under the pile of dirt, lay the body of a cold, lifeless thing.

These memories don't leave your brain. They burn an image that will remain there for years to come and the more you think about it, the more vivid it is.

These memories are tiring. They will leave scars in your brain and they will never leave you alone. Though I try to explain my story to others, they often ask me to show them the remains and evidence of the countless amounts of traumatizing events that have happened to me over the years; sadly, there is no proof to show them.

I can slowly tell and explain my story to them, but I don't have a scar to show them. It's hard getting up every day. The very thought of going to take a shower will exhaust those who are both physically and mentally drained.

In order to survive, people will go to great lengths to do what is necessary to continue thriving and living in the community that they are so widely known for all their selfless acts. They are living in communities that people hundreds of years ago built together.

In the end, when it comes to it, they would rather save themselves than save others in communities which they have built.

Most times, we need to escape and flee away from situations we put ourselves in out of desperation while other times, other people's selfishness overcomes them.

Even the kindest of people will be overcome with emotions so great that they will simply do what it takes to get rid of those who they dislike.

If you put salt all over someone's body, many animals such as goats can and will come take every opportunity they have to go lick it off; however, that's not enough to satisfy its needs.

It'll keep licking until eventually, it comes down to the flesh and even then, it will remain enjoying the tangy flavor of the salt.

They'll keep going until one day, there is nothing left of you other than a decaying, rotten corpse with a smell so strong, people don't dare come near it.

In the end, your organs start to slowly decompose, insects will slowly make their way inside every possible nook and corner they can find and eat away at the sweet taste of your blood-soaked organs.

It is a cruel ending for anyone to go through. Cruelty caused by humans towards other humans who are in need of any sort of validation they can get.

Although I put a lot of pride in my work and successes, most times it's hard to articulate and recognize the realities and limitations of the criminal justice system.

You slowly earn the respect of the illustrious prosecutors and the judges, who you will be working with repeatedly for many years to come.

Who knows what may come of this diary, perhaps a gold medal, a noble award or maybe it may lead to my name being printed on many history books honoring me for my work.

I don't know what, but I expect something great to come of this book.

A book where perhaps secrets and lies, which appear serious to human kind, may just be a grain of sand on a beach.

A beach with so many grains of sand that if it were liquid-like, the sand would slowly eat away at people's organs as they yearn and plead for even the littlest of mercy.

I never realized it would lead to my downfall.

One thing for sure, being a detective isn't easy. Having to see families being full of joy the first day and the next, everything they had would be torn apart from them in a flash.

When I started this job, almost five years ago, I never realized how traumatizing almost all of the events in my job would lead me to be. This job is not for the weak-hearted, poor-spirited and the cowards out there. It helps loads of people, but sometimes I wonder who will help us.

Perhaps that's why during the morning, I may seem full of life and ready to put those who deserve it behind bars but at night, I hide my *sadness and misery* away as I'm drowning in alcohol and hiding myself among women.

To be a detective, you need to make sure you're a convincing person. Who knows how many times you'll have to lie and say:

"Everything will be alright."

Knowing nothing is how it appears or seems to be. You have to be ready to view the sight of dark crimson blood slowly dripping down a person's bashed head, and the scrapes and bruises shown all over their body knowing they are all self-defense wounds.

You have to be ready to see a young person commit suicide over not having enough money to pay off a loan, their hesitation, their second thoughts and their regret once their finger hits that trigger as their face is covered in hot agony as tears run down their face and their family runs to see what made such a loud noise.

Apply pressure. Apply pressure. Apply pressure.

The only words that are repeated in my head over and over again as all we can do is hope for their survival and pray that their deadly bleeding will eventually stop, that they'll be able to make it long enough for the surgeons to save them.

A part of me will always be and remain in all those moments where I, along with everyone else at the crime scene, was hopeless and all we could do was contain ourselves. The part when their skin slowly got greyer as time went past and their eyes that were once filled with sparkle and brightness, became more and more dull.

The moment in which their soul had crossed the border will forever haunt me. A part of me can't let go of all the people whose lives were lost. Seeing the sight of real blood is nothing like watching a movie with blood pouring down. It's just like how real death is nothing like movie death.

There is no amount of time that can prepare anyone with all the horror that will be sprung onto them the moment they see a cold body laying down on the floor. During this time, all the learning that I had prepared for times like these, goes away, bit by bit.

One minute I was holding their hands, reassuring them that everything would be okay, and the next, I was sitting applying pressure to their head trying to keep their skull in one piece, at least until the ambulance arrived.

At that moment, I knew that there was no hope left, I knew that we were saying goodbye.

Though I didn't know those who I helped, I knew that they were human just like me. I locked my eyes into their eyes and tried to give them one last moment of warmth, as I was bathed in the pool of their blood. Until their desperate heavy breathing was eventually no longer heard.

Though I knew they had departed, I was still sitting in a pool of cold blood, hugging them as if they were still here somewhere. I sat there emotionless. I couldn't bear to move and let them go. This is the kind of horror that you wouldn't wish upon anyone, *not even your worst enemy*.

They all slip into deep darkness, not only the dead, but also those who have to live with the grief.

In the end, silence.

Silence has roamed the earth. Its dark spirits have been set loose, out of their strapping leash until eventually, they attack and invade all of mankind. They invade even the most admirable of people, those who everyone loves.

Knowing all that, I still survive. I still get up every day and go to work. Without knowing what mysteries I will encounter next.

Sometimes I wonder why humans had to invent things like jobs. Why couldn't we just live in peace? Why do we need man-made things such as money to "buy" things such as food – a human necessity? After all, in simple words, we all live on a floating rock in the middle of nowhere.

Don't get me wrong, being a 23-year-old man living alone can be quite a thrilling experience. The freedom that comes with it, and the fact that you can go home and come back at any time you please without having someone waiting for you is worry-free. However, it does get lonely realizing that you're by yourself.

We'll never know for sure why someone may decide to end their life voluntarily or rather how many people in total decide to end their life.

Perhaps they got someone else to do it for them and they've never been caught or maybe they were never found by anyone.

Their bodies are left to rot and eventually perish and disappear out of existence.

In the end, the family will eventually give up all hope in finding answers as they realize there's no hope left.

We live in a two-faced world full of deception that has led the younger generations to believe certain behaviors are okay because of how normalized they have become.

Now, children who are currently in elementary school are obsessed with technology and will rarely be seen without using it.

You can find devices being used in most schools and although it can be helpful at times, technology can be like a poison.

It was made to spread illness and slowly let people suffer rather than killing them quickly. A little bit of it and even those with a strong moral foundation can be led astray. It is a living nightmare. Use it wisely for you may come to regret it soon.

You may be wondering, who are the main targets of a poison so deadly that not even the bravest will dare to go near? The ugly truth is that everyone is the target, poison was made to act as an efficient virus, to spread illness across the world slowly rather than to kill everyone fast.

A few drops here and there and the decay will eventually set in. A terrible survival journey for those affected.

Those affected by it may have survived, but one thing for sure is that once even the littlest of it enters your system, you will forever live with it.

I myself have seen it happen to people, both physically and mentally.

I had come back to work a couple months later after leaving, and was hopeful that I wouldn't decide to leave again. The reason why I had come back was mainly because over the last few months, all I could think about was how much fun and thrill I used to have being a detective.

Who knows what secrets lie in every crime scene? What I was going to find was going to be different every single time.

That's what I enjoyed most about being a detective.

Now enough about that, let's start solving, finding and helping those who need all the support they can get.

I sped through the damp streets and rushed home, hoping to catch Isabella, my wife, before she fully packed and left me. I just wanted to see her one last time, even though I was secretly hoping she would've left already. I didn't want to go through the pain once again.

The engine's rumble beneath me marked how urgent this was and how it had to be done now, otherwise I would be too scared to confront her later on.

As I pulled into the driveway, a silent plea ran through my head. All I could think about was the remaining moments I had left with Isabella.

Could it possibly be enough to somehow convince her to stay?

After everything she had said, would she still want to stay?

As I stepped through the doorway of our home, I rushed around trying to look for Isabella. The familiar surroundings around me seemed comforting, yet at the same time so suffocating.

Was anything missing? Had she taken her things yet to leave?

As I walked into our living room, knots started forming in my stomach as I saw Isabella sitting down on the worn-out couch, with a sea of packed boxes and bags surrounding her.

The amount of bags and how big they all were proved that this wasn't something small.

Rather, she had packed her whole life into three large suitcases and a couple of boxes.

I stood there still, waiting for her to say something. Yet all I got was a room of silence, filled with a bunch of unsaid words and unshared emotions that hung in the air, waiting for someone to start talking.

It almost felt like the room was starting to sigh, being a silent witness to the chapter of our story that was coming to an end.

In the midst of raw desperation, I swallowed the lump that was in my throat and started talking,

"Isabella, plea—"

Isabella quickly cut me off,

"Noah, you know how hard this is for me, right?"

I gulped before I answered, "Isabella, I know, believe me. But haven't we been through so much together? Don't you remember the day we first met? The way you looked at me, like I was the only person standing in the room?"

She mumbled, "Obviously I remember. I haven't forgotten about you, Noah. But things have changed. *You've* changed."

I stood there, quiet.

She wasn't wrong about any of that. What was I meant to do? Beg and plead for her to stay? I know it's best this way but I just can't seem to let go.

The memories of our journey together flashed before my eyes and the badge I wore as a detective faded into insignificance. I felt so vulnerable around her.

It was even worse now, since the room felt suspended in time. Every second I stood in front of her felt like an eternity.

I snapped at her, "Why did you have to stay here? Why did you have to wait for me to come back? Was it to say goodbye? Why didn't you just leave straight away?"

I sighed.

She looked away from me, raising her trembling hand to her face, wiping away the tears that my words had caused.

She took a few breaths and then started looking at me once more. This time, the blue depths in her eyes seemed to hold a quiet promise of healing amidst the turmoil we were in.

Looking into her eyes, I uttered, "Isabella, I'm sorry. I know that it's best this way. I'm just going to miss you, and I don't know what I'll do without you."

She placed her hand on my shoulder, before leaning in for a hug.

"You'll be okay, Noah. But I'm sorry. I just can't seem to make it work anymore. Please be safe for me."

She gathered her bags and started walking out of the door. Before leaving, she looked back at me and mumbled, "Goodbye, Noah."

I couldn't respond to her.

All I could do was watch as she got into her car and drove away, fast.

As if she was waiting for this moment for a while.

I quickly rushed upstairs and took off my shoes before creeping onto my bed. I was alone. It was all my fault. What was I meant to do?

Tears quickly slipped from my eyes and there was nothing I could do to fight back. I simply laid down and allowed them to keep going.

In the shadows of the night, the weight of despair that I had felt had become too heavy to bear. Slowly, I took my hand and placed them into my pockets.

I reached for the bottle that I had found on my desk earlier that day that had held a temporary solace in it.

The cold surface of the pills provided a cooling feeling to my hands as I held it while thinking about what it was that I was about to do. Yet, I was filled with nothing but desperation.

I grabbed a couple of pills from the bottle and swallowed them one by one. Their bitter taste was a constant reminder of everything that had happened in my life. Before I could start to do anything, the room seemed to start blurring and the numbness had set in.

Falling down on the floor, I crawled onto the bed and jumped on it. As I laid down, the room around me faded into a distant echo. The rhythm of my heart grew slower and slower. Was this how it felt like to die?

The darkness crept in. It almost felt like a soothing embrace that offered me an escape from the ache that constantly consumed me.

It didn't take long for my vision to completely go away and eventually, I slipped away, even if it was for a little while.

Chapter 2.
A Crime Has Taken Place

A series of banging vibrations woke me up in a startle. I sprung out of bed, or well, rolled and slammed my head on the corner of my nightstand.

Oh, god, I thought, clutching at my pounding head while trying to stagger up.

Everything that I had done the previous night came rushing back. A disoriented fog descended, leaving me suspended in a haze of pure shock and uncertainty. The line between intention and impulse started to confuse me.

Did I really try to end my own life?

Was it just nothing but a desperate cry for help?

This wasn't the first time that I had taken my antidepressants since this whole week, it feels like it's all I've been doing.

While clutching at my pounding head, the realization that I may never know my own intentions was a chilling reminder of the depths my pain had taken me to.

My room felt surreal, as if I was peering through a distorted lens into a world not familiar to me. I couldn't recognize where anything was. Was I even at my house?

I wasn't. My house wasn't a home without Isabella.
I tried to find a paper towel to quickly take care of the pain that I was feeling in my head.

I was late for work, and one quick glance at the clock had confirmed that. I had had the same recurring nightmare that has kept me awake at night and when I finally managed to get some sleep, it would only be for an hour.

I knew that it was getting bad, again. Something had to be done about it, but I had no time.

It was like my head had a separate heart of its own that would pound whenever it felt like it, and although I was dizzy, I got up quickly and hobbled over towards the mirror.

The bedside table was sharp enough to cut flesh as if it posed no resistance.

I quickly rushed over to the bathroom and got a towel from the sink and started wiping the crimson blood, but no matter how much pressure I applied, the blood still kept gushing onto the towel.

The cold blood that kept coming out of my head seemed to glisten in the dim light, which posed as an unsettling reminder for my past.

I took the towel off while glaring at my reflection through the mirror.

It didn't stop. From the raw wound, I could see the scarlet rivulets flowing, each little droplet tracing an uncharted path down the skin. The sight was both unsettling and weirdly fascinating. It was a reminder to me about how each of these little droplets was flowing inside of me.

Keeping me alive.

Hearing my phone ringing outside on my nightstand, I was shaken back to reality. I quickly snapped back and put the towel back on the wound.

I rushed outside to pick up the call. I realized that my boss was calling. I answered.

"Hey, I know I'm la—"

I winced in a strained voice, as I was in pain.

My boss, Marcus, bitterly responded, "This is the second time this week, Noah. You've just come back after taking a six-month-long leave. You really need to come in earlier."

"I know, and I apologize for that,"

I mumbled in a distressed tone.

Before I knew it, Marcus had already hung up the phone.

At that moment, I had already known that he was smirking as I knew that when I reached work, he'd be able to insult and belittle me once again.

As I looked over at the mirror once again, I saw that the once bright red spot on my head had now begun to darken as the wound clotted.

I had recently come back to work after being suspended for almost six months.

My job keeps me busy. We work for at least eight hours at once without realizing. However, a good thing is, time flies when you know what you're doing may help and protect those who need it.

It was perfect for me though. I needed a distraction away from reality: away from all the chaos that had happened in my life.

I barely had any free time for myself. Life was playing on repeat every single day; wake up, go to work, come back home, and repeat.

After a while, it gets boring, it gets tiring, it weakens you and wears you out but what can you do? You just have to live with it.

Not all people decide to live with it though, 47,646 people *every year in America* decide not to anyways.

Today was the first time in weeks that I felt like I could actually accomplish something out of my day. Usually, life is just a cycle that keeps on repeating until you simply pass away. I would always wake up, that's if I even managed to get any sleep in me. Then I would head off to work.

It drained me to the point where it was unbearable and a break from work was inevitable.

I returned just a week ago. I had already known that it was a bad idea. For generations people have and continued to employ people at starvation levels, yet everyone continues to work for them as if it were top dollar.

Standing still, with my head still pounding from the immense force it had felt, I realized that I wouldn't be able to work all day in this condition. I hobbled out to my room, and called my boss.

I quickly said, "Hey, Marcus. I won't be able to make it in today. I feel really dizzy. My head is pounding."

He replied with a chuckle before answering, "Fine. Suit yourself. Have fun at home."

He hung up.

I stood amidst the scattered papers and dim glow near my desk in my room. I realized that something in my room had changed. Within the walls, an unsettling feeling looms around, casting a shadow over a haven of comfort.

I didn't want to be home anymore, but what was I supposed to do? Show up at work after telling my boss I was taking a day off? I had a yearning feeling of getting something done, yet I had no clue in the world about what had to be done.

I started gazing at my wardrobe and all the clothing options blurred and I grabbed whatever was within my reach before layering them on. I started to button up my shirt, while forgetting some buttons along the way.

I slipped my shoes on without any consideration for matching my outfit.

I rushed downstairs and grabbed my keys, stuffing everything down whatever pockets I found. As I got into my car, I sat there, not knowing what it was I was doing there.

Embracing spontaneity, I put my foot on the pedal and began driving, my head still throbbing in pain from earlier. The open road stretched out before me, laying down many promising journeys for me.

I had no fixed destination in mind, so all I did was drive until I couldn't.

The clock and the miles started ticking and time quickly lost its grip. I found myself sitting in my car in front of a church.

The moon's feeble light casted a ghostly pallor over the facade, and the windows of the church felt like empty eyes staring back at me. I got out of my car and closed the door.

Every footstep I took across the uneven ground echoed in the void. Was I alone? As I sat down, an overwhelming sense of solitude enveloped me, almost feeling like it had put a mask over me. Trapping me of all oxygen.

I was wishing to purify myself from everything wrong I had ever done throughout my life. I was wishing for someone to forgive my sins because I couldn't forgive myself.

What had I done that was so terrible?

I was good at my job as a detective, but it truly ruined me as a person. I couldn't even keep one stable relationship.

How bad had it gotten? Was all hope for me too far gone?

I found myself laying down on the pew bench and suddenly seeking refuge in the embrace of the dim lights. The weight of my worries only seemed to meld with the darkness in the room.

Lying down, I started to sink into a pew of weariness that only seemed to overtake me. Exhaustion from life itself made me want to lay down forever. With each soft breath I took, the flickers of the candlelight shone before my eyes and my consciousness soon drifted into dreams.

I suddenly felt like this church was a cocoon of solace. The only place where the weight of stress dissolved into the quietude that I needed. I fell asleep right there on the spot.

As I crossed the only known barrier between the living and the dead, the boundaries of reality began to blur, and I started to reconnect with someone I once held very dear to me. Their presence alone makes me feel an overwhelming feeling of happiness. Every one of their laughter made my heart beat faster and faster.

I was so grateful for the chance to once again hold Isabella close, just like I used to. Even if it was only in the realms of sleep.

Soon, the echoes of my dreams faded and were replaced by the insistent vibration of my phone, jolting me back from the dead.

I fumbled through my pocket to find my phone and saw an incoming call from Marcus.

I answered.

"Noah, you have to come here now. Something happened and we need you."

Marcus insisted in a worried tone.

"Okay, I'll be right there."

I replied, anxious by what just happened.

I started sprinting down the church hallways and closed the heavy wooden door behind me before I left. The streetlights casted shadows on the pavement as I made my way to my car that I parked nearby. I realized that I had been asleep for a while. Was it the guilt of not being able to forgive myself for prioritizing my job?

The memory I had of the church's tranquility simply lingered in the background and all I could think was to keep on driving to my workplace. It wasn't far from the church.

As I arrived, I parked my car and picked up my coat before running to the large doors. What was so important that demanded my attention on my day off? I was so confused.

As I entered through the doors, I immediately spotted Marcus, surrounded by many other detectives nearby.

"Marcus. What happened?"

I stated, hoping he would give me some insight.

"Just, come watch."

Marcus insisted with a distressed look on his face.

He picked up the remote we used to capture any security footage we needed around town and proceeded to hit play.

As I watched the footage being played to me, I felt a mixture of dread and disbelief. A familiar figure on the screen was being shot to death by her boyfriend. The more I watched, the more time seemed to slow and I could feel the gravity of the situation hanging heavy in the air.

Sirens wailed in the distance, in a desperate attempt to save her. Strangers became witnesses to a nightmare as their faces were etched with shock and horror and they watched the ambulance dump her body in a body bag.

My unease quickly deepened into a chilling realization. The footage played in a loop, forever haunting me with their repetition that sketched an image into my mind.

The security footage captured more than anything I could have imagined; it captured more than just an act of destruction towards another human. It had captured Isabella being brutally murdered on the screen.

My heart started racing. It was getting harder and harder to breathe.

"Noah, it wasn't your fault. We already caught who did it. It was her boyfriend. They got into some sort of an argument."

Marcus insisted, putting his now warm hand over my shoulders and leaning in for a hug.

I let him. I couldn't think straight. A mixture of confusion, anger and sadness overwhelmed me.

I stormed towards the interrogation room, knowing that Isabella's killer would still be there. Once I opened the door, I grabbed him.

"How could you do that?"

I repeated multiple times.

He didn't answer. Marcus got me off of him and had me sit in my office to cool off. He left, knowing I needed to be alone.

Grief has a way of removing you from the world and the only way to get back into it is if you've got real strength.

You'll find yourself retracing the steps of the past, trying to make sense of the events that led to you being there right then.

Grief's shock is like an internal storm, nothing less than that. A turmoil that rages silently while the rest of the world keeps going as if nothing around us happened.

As if nothing around us changed.

But in reality, it was as if a part of me had been torn away, leaving an empty void inside of me. A chasm that nothing in life could ever fill.

That was when I realized that from now on, the simplest of tasks will become a challenge. I'll forever have a physical sensation printed on me that weighs heavy on the chest and slows the beat of my heart.

The noises around me seemed distant and muffled. A seismic jolt that fractured the very foundation of my existence. In a single moment, the world began shifting on its axis, leaving me all alone, having to deal with the surreal state of reality and disbelief.

I felt an odd sense of detachment away from reality, as if my own feelings weren't really mine.

As if they were being filtered through a foggy lens.

I could see Marcus' distorted figure in front of me, waiting for me to say something. Anything.

I began to speak,

"Marcus, plea—"

A sudden sensation surged from the pit of my stomach, a sickly feeling as if an invisible hand was clenching at my core.

My words caught in my throat and I had to bear the consequence of this suffocating grip being forced on me.

I bent down on the floor, while facing the garbage can and the contents of my being expelled.

An emotional weight momentarily silenced my voice and settled in the pit of my stomach like a cloud that obscures all clarity of thoughts.

Marcus saw everything and began to order, "Noah, go home. You shouldn't stay here in this state."

He looked at me with a look of pity, as if he really felt the pain I was feeling and understood it.

I could never look at that church I spent my time in the same ever again. How could such a place allow something so terrible to happen to someone else?

Without talking to Marcus, or even thanking him for how he would handle the situation, I walked out and sat down in my car for a while. At that moment, I had found myself trapped in a suffocating cycle of pain and despair. The church was now a place that became a symbol of my internal turmoil. A place which was supposed to offer solace and hope.

Isabella was the sweetest soul I had ever known. Her eyes were a shade of blue that would mirror the beautiful boundless skies on a clear summer day.

The more I kept closing my eyes, the more the memories rushed back to me.

The more I found myself caught in the delicate threads of nostalgia.

Her blue eyes were framed by the soft curve of her lashes, which spoke in volumes without words. Sharing multiple stories of laughter, dreams and a constant reminder of our connection.

A reminder of a time where innocence and purity danced in perfect harmony, wrapped within the delicate feelings of the sweetest girl I'd ever known.

I remained seated in the car, with my head resting on the head rest. I began driving to my home as I couldn't bear the thought of being anywhere near the precinct where I worked.

As I sped away, I began calling one of the people I relied on the most, my therapist.

She picked up.

She asked, "Hey, Noah. Is everything alright?"

I started mumbling, my voice clearly shaken, "Yes. I just needed to hear someone's voice, I'm so sorry. I just got the worst news of my life."

She responded, "Noah, it's all right. You can always call me, you don't have to ever apologize for needing someone."

Smiling, I answered, "Yes, yes. Thank you. I'll call you back later. I really appreciate this."

I hung up the phone.

At this point, I was pulling over to my driveway and sped upstairs to rest.

However, as I sat in my car, I felt my phone vibrating through my back pocket. The city lights dimmed in the background and it managed to cast a shadow over the worn-out pavement. Hesitating, I answered my phone that had disrupted the silence that enveloped me.

With reluctance, I spoke, "Hello, Who is this?"

A soft voice answered back at me, "It's Alice. We used to know each other from high school."

Oh god. My heart quickened as I heard her mention her name. A mixture of emotions went through me. It was a name that I hadn't thought about in years yet was filled with joy and awkwardness.

A mix of surprise and apprehension quickly tightened my tone as I repeated, "Alice."

Her voice continued, "Yeah. Hey, I know this is totally last minute but I am having a get together with everyone else and we heard about what happened. You're welcome to join. I'll text you the details."

Shocked, I quickly answered, "Yeah, I'd love that thanks. I'll be on my way now."

She hung up.

The unexpected connection with a past I had unintentionally distanced myself from. For so long, it felt as if I had no one surrounding me. I was a solitary figure navigating my way through life with a deliberate detachment. The memories of what had happened that day still lingered in the back of my mind but I finally had something to look forward to.

Once again, I remained seated in my car and began speeding my way to the location.

As I drove, I could see a man pass under the fluorescent glare of a street lamp. His face quickly became a shifting mosaic. I could see the heat from his mouth creating smoky plumes of steam as he was whistling a song. A twisted grin tugged at the corners of my lips as I observed the man's choreography with fascination.

Grief comes to me in waves. With time, the sharp stings will lessen and will let the good memories flood in instead. I mourn the loss of someone I've never met because I never felt like Isabella could be who she wanted to be around me. Being with me meant she had to make sacrifices.

I mourn the loss of her life and the loss of myself for I was left behind in the home we built together.

As I arrived, I quickly hopped out of my car and stood in front of the house before entering. I didn't know what to expect.

I hesitated, caught in the fleeting pause before unlocking the door. My hand adhered to the frigid metal of the handle and I was unsure whether I was ready to meet up with people just yet.

Inhaling deeply, I steeled myself before entering. The seductive pulsations of music that came from inside of the house enticed me with their rhythmic allure.

As I stepped inside, I could recognize Alice straight away. It seemed like her features had been frozen in time from six years ago.

With the low hum of the conversations and the rhythmic beat of the music, our eyes finally met. I started walking towards her.

"Alice?" I uttered surprisingly, as this whole evening was totally unexpected.

She turned for a moment, "Yes it's me," she replied, a soft smile playing on her lips. "You made it!"

"It's been a long time. You look the same," I sighed, relieved by her warmth.

A gentle laugh escaped her lips, "Well almost the same. Time leaves its mark, doesn't it?"

I nodded, acutely aware of the unspoken history between us.

After reconnecting with some of my old friends, it felt like though we hadn't talked in a long time, we still knew each other. After everything that had happened to me lately, this felt like a breath of fresh air.

The air buzzed with laughter as we all exchanged stories that made up for lack of communication between us for the past few years. The more conversations we had, the more we felt like time kept speeding away.

As the night wore on, I decided that it was time to get going and sped away in my car back home.

Arriving home, I quickly rushed to open the door and went to my room.

As I lay there on my back, with my eyes gazed at the ceiling, I felt enveloped in a surreal detachment from reality, a sensation that washed over me like a numbing tide. I tried to grapple with the ebb and flow of my emotions, longing to return back to the reality I felt so distant from. Everybody else around me was here, yet there I was, floating adrift in a sea of uncertainty.

The ceiling was a canvas for my thoughts. I was here, yet not quite here. I only felt like an observer from afar and not anything like a participant.

In this odd detachment, I started drifting away, with the softness of my bed calling me in to dream. I listened to it.

The alarm I had set kept vibrating on my bedside table. I sat up straight on my bed and quickly turned it off. I began to simply stare at the blank wall in front of me.

Suddenly, I gained back all my senses and that's when I glanced over back at the bedside table. I had noticed the old bottle of pills that I had gotten prescribed from my doctor.

I could see the dust it was collecting from the lack of touch. I hesitated as I leaned in closer to get it but before I realized, I had grabbed it and poured a handful into my mouth.

I rushed to get some water and gulped it down as quickly as I could.

I reached for my phone and that's when I realized I had gotten another phone call. This time it was from one of my best friends and my co-worker, Liam. I quickly answered as I sat up straight on my bed.

"Noah, you need to get here fast," he stated quickly.

I worriedly replied, "Liam? Liam, what's going on? I don't understand Lia—"

He had hung up the phone, promptly cutting me off.

A pressure surrounded me and closed in on me like two metal jaws. I let out a quick breath in an attempt to soothe the worried shake in my limbs.

At that moment, that's when I realized that one of my best friends could be in some serious danger. Danger is a stoplight that you never knew could be so serious, it's when you need to trust yourself when all you can think of is doubt.

I quickly sprung out of bed and picked up the first thing I saw off the floor and started putting it on. I carelessly tucked my shirt in and sprinted out into my car.

Thinking about it, I realize that I may have forgotten to do the most basic of things, locking my door behind me. It was something I had never forgotten to do.

I sped down the empty roads with my only thought being how I needed to get there as soon as I could. I needed to find out what was going on.

Once I arrived at the precinct and slowly got closer, I found that all the workers were all standing still staring at something. It was a board filled with threatening messages to everyone, including the boss himself.

It was disturbing reading the signs, and the more I examined it, it kept getting worse. I quickly let out a big sigh as I realized it wasn't anything. It wasn't serious since anyone could have done it. They could have done it as a sick prank.

"Somebody here has betrayed all of us, and I will find out who it is," Marcus snapped, his gaze sharply sweeping the room.

"Calm down. I'm sure this is some sort of prank, a joke perhaps," I quickly tried to reason.

"If it was a prank, why would one of our own detective's go missing the same day this happened?" Marcus screeched indignantly.

I started to feel uneasy.

"What? Who went missing? I'm so confus—"

"GO HOME, since you can't even seem to show up for work on time anymore," Marcus indignantly snarled before aggressively shoving me aside as he went stomping out of the room.

I didn't go home. He didn't realize that I didn't come to work because of how mortified I was these past few months.

After being fired by Marcus, he eventually realized that the way he treated almost everyone was wrong, not because he was a good person, but because he had gotten in trouble with someone higher-up than him.

I was numb. I couldn't feel anything. The whole point of my job was to help others, please others, and satisfy others.

How was I supposed to help them when I couldn't help myself?

All the people who came to us had absolutely nothing after they realized one of their loved ones had passed away. They felt as if they had no safety, no right to food or home.

No place to go. When I was with them, no matter what I did, it didn't seem to help. Rather all they felt was judged and insecure.

As I looked around the precinct, I suddenly spotted a case file on top of the countless pages of missing person cases, left there abandoned, collecting dust until someone finally bothered to pick it up. The one on the top was different, it wasn't like all the other ones. This person was an important figure in society.

I slowly approached the paper and started reading it.

The paper read:

"Charlotte Thomas – a famous scientist who had been working on finding the cure to cancer disappeared from her lab, but was later found brutally stabbed in her own lab."

It was quite disturbing reading those lines. Who would have anything against a great woman who was willing to sacrifice her whole life and time to find a cure to a deadly disease?

As I kept reading on, I shockingly found the reason why no one claimed to have seen anything was because she didn't die in her lab.

Someone, or rather *something* had moved her body there to send a message.

My mind thought of all kinds of ways she could've been killed. How a remorseless killer had made sure her last minutes alive were the worst. Her life was flashing through her eyes as she *gasped* and *screamed* for help as her life was being bled out of the multiple stab wounds.

She died trying to find a cure for something so serious. How could someone take that away from her? In the future, anyone who would get struck by cancer would be able to get a second chance. They would be filled with satisfaction of perhaps finding a way out.

Who would do such a thing? Who was desperate enough to steal her life's work?

It was someone inhuman and wicked. It was done on purpose.

I've always made sure that those who **tormented** others and made their lives miserable would pay for it. After all, it is what everyone else expects of me. I hated murderers. They are the roots of all evil and are the extensions of demons.

They have ruined many lives because of their careless actions and therefore, should pay. Most of them rot behind prison cells as the stench of sewage travels throughout the concrete walls.

For the rest of their lives, they spend it wishing they could turn back and **never get caught** for their dirty sins. While others get to cherish and enjoy their long life after taking someone else's life. They never get any punishment, whether these people have been caught for their crimes or not.

This is the part I dreaded the most about my job. It was the fact that we had to go to the place of the crime, even if it's gloomy outside and the sun was nowhere to be found, we still had to search the place of the crime.

Though people considered me **'brave'**, they didn't realize that if all I had was no fear then it would've been useless for me to be brave.

I realize that the more scared and frightened I am, then perhaps it might give me an insight seeing how normal I truly am that it might bolster me into being somewhat of what today's society considers a **'brave'** person.

The way I see it, there is no such thing as having *'bad luck'*. Some people simply don't try at all and simply rely on luck.

They believe that even their bad luck becomes great luck almost instantly. They believe that anything that brings them solace and joy in life are lucky charms.

People aren't *'unlucky'* for meeting a certain individual. That person was once their favorite person. Each person has a journey and a different story.

Some, however, have their lives taken and stripped away from them too soon by people who they thought were close to them.

People who they thought they could trust.

Before making my way to the crime scene, I had to make sure I knew what I was in for. Who knows what filthy lies and mysteries would lie deep beneath the blood and fingerprints? Perhaps a body, *a deceased one*. A body that fought so hard to stay alive, only to find out that they weren't powerful enough.

I had to find out every last detail about the deceased scientist: Charlotte Thomas. Perhaps *what* she was known for prior to her work in science. *Who* did she know before she started her career? Did they want to be like her, or did they want *to be her*?

Jealousy eats people up from deep within until they are nothing but a zombie corpse, feasting on the hive-mind. They try to find every opportunity they can to ruin someone, and to ruin their life's work.

For jealousy, there is no cloak of invisibility covering and hiding all of its evil roots, rather it is much easier to spot. I myself have found my mind wandering around all kinds of thoughts. One of them being jealousy. There is no escape from it, since it haunts everyone.

As I was trying my best to keep my breathing stable, the loud vibrations coming from my phone distracted me. It was another call from *'Liam'*. I quickly answered.

When I accepted the call, Liam's voice was not the voice who greeted me.

"Hey. Hello? Are you there? I'll text you more details and information about the murder. You already know what happened. Your mind just can't seem to accept it."

"Liam? What are you talki—" I was cut off by a loud beep, indicating he had hung up.

An immense amount of text messages kept piling up, one after the other. Each explaining different aspects of her life: where she was before she was ruthlessly attacked, who was with her, and who were the suspects. It was so much information to process.

Finally packing up, I gripped the steering wheel and my hands trembled as the car surged forward. My heart pounded in sync with the car's speed. The road stretched endlessly before me and each passing streetlight only ended up casting fleeting glimpses of the turmoil that was etched onto my face. As I reached my house, I let out a sigh. Ready to get inside and wash this horrible day off me.

As I looked outside, the once clear sunny day had been taken over by a dark fog; just when I thought I would be able to get things done, I quickly knew I couldn't. I helplessly threw my body across my couch and laid down staring at the ceiling, thinking about life as a whole.

My thoughts scattered around like lost fragments of a shattered mirror. My mind came across unfamiliar landscapes I never thought I'd delve into. Each little broken shard unraveled a tapestry of emotions; a thread woven into the fabric of my being.

That is what confusion is, and that's all I was as my mind grappled for answers.

I got up and made a cup of coffee. At least it would help me remain calm until I am able to process all of those text messages.

Working as a detective was not easy. It took a lot of time just for one case and in the end, whenever you finish the case, you never get recognized for it. It was complicated making sure your assumptions and accusations were accurate.

A good detective is able to see and detect the clues and logic behind every little thing. Even those little things that go unnoticed by the everyday eye however, a great detective is able to immerse themselves with the perfect balance of their emotional needs and the needs of the social aspect needed to start to make life better, for others and themselves.

Any mistakes would lead to lots of trouble. After all, to catch a criminal you have to ***think like one***.

My mind could easily go from one thing to another, from understanding to desperate and grappling for answers.

By the time I was done, it was one in the afternoon, and I was ready.

I had already made sure to contact all those that would be working with me on this case.

"Hey, you ready?"

I shot a text to the first one before jumping over to another contact.

"Looking forward to getting back to work with you."

I quickly typed out before pressing send.

I put on my black broad-brimmed hat and slipped into my black shoes that I had recently just got. To top it all off, I placed a coat on my shoulders. It was one typical, basic outfit.

But to me, we detectives are all the same. We are all paranoid freaks who can't blend into any place looking normal even if our lives depended on it.

I carefully traced my steps as I slowly made my way towards the crime scene. It was not too far away. I would often go near this place a lot, especially during the night time.

I had been so obsessed and so attracted to this place. For some odd reason, it gave me an overwhelming sensation of peace. Lately, I had started staying away from this place, though.

I would often find myself falling asleep, only to realize that my nightmares had been haunted and visited by one horrific site. This place, the abandoned graveyard.

Was I crazy for this? Most likely, yes.

Being here was pounding a sickening reminder through my mind, of memories I tried so hard to forget.

That one ***pitch black*** night, where the air was cold and the raindrops pelted to the ground. The only thing that kept me warm was the blood still managing to pump through my veins.

I was awake yet not awake. My body was asleep yet my mind was wandering. I could feel myself running throughout the place. Running away from someone, *something.* What was it? I didn't know.

Perhaps I was running away from this cruel world that we live in.

Once I arrived at the crime scene, I carefully examined the area, looking for every little detail. The details that the average eye seems to ignore. The entire process is both simple and complicated at the same time.

If you wanted to question those who witnessed the crime, you wouldn't get much. Possibly even nothing. It all happens so fast, so unexpectedly.

"They were tall, or possibly medium height. They had black hair, or possibly brown hair."

I took one quick glance at everything before I started browsing for any evidence proving that a murder had happened and an innocent life was taken away.

While I wandered through the lab, I immediately saw that it had been trashed. There were items strewn about the place with glass shards sprayed across the floor, the fragments glittering against the tiled floor.

It got me wondering and thinking about all the different scenarios that could've happened to cause this.

Without me realizing, I had leaned on the table and accidentally dropped one of the glass tubes. Before my brain could register the sound of breaking glass, my eyes immediately shut tight ensuring that nothing entered my eyes.

I froze, trying to process everything that had just happened.

Everything but my mind remained statue-like. All I could think about when I finally allowed my eyelids to flutter themselves open was how horrible the shattering sound was.

When I saw that the ground next to my feet was stained red and trailed over to the carpet it leaked out from, I was confused.

Only for a moment before I realized it was most likely Charlotte's and not my own.

When I managed to look away from the blood, I met Marcus's gaze.

"Are you okay?" he asked quietly.

I quickly assured him.

"Yeah, I'm okay, thank you."

Yet, how could I be okay?

I looked back over to Charlotte's body. It was sprawled across the floor and looked cold with sickly pale skin. I shoved down the pain and trauma this caused out of my mind.

Dead people are thought to be nothing but skeletons once the spark that they once had passed on.

Dead people, dead animals, are meat and as we treat our dead with respect and marvel, perhaps it makes us find new respect and appreciation for our fellow friends around us.

Possibly, there may have been a terrible argument which had happened before the murder. Perhaps someone had gotten angry and hostile during one fight. One fight that could've ended if one of them had just moved on. Instead, ***they killed her***.

Could it have been a robbery?

Someone who was jealous of her success decided to murder her? There were so many guesses that I think all had an equal possibility of happening. They all deserve my attention, no matter what.

The more I thought about it, the more I thought that perhaps someone had found the cure to cancer ***first***. If so, they could've been the one to easily do this to her. They could've been the one who gave her a ***brutal ending***.

Some people say, "No matter what, always take your secrets to your grave."

However, I think that at times, **secrets take you to your grave**. They suffocate and swelter every single person until carefully, one by one, the secrets they so desperately tried to keep, spill carelessly like paint.

Secrets draw and point out what each person thinks about. Their thoughts, their mind, their brain.

What they truly believe in their hearts. The darker the secrets are, the harder they are to contain within themselves.

All I could think about was whether or not someone had a secret so big, they decided to kill someone (Charlotte) for it.

Though everything was out of its place, there was nothing missing. The drawer, which contained all the pipettes, syringes and droppers, was opened yet it was all dumped out of its place.

The microscopes in the lab were thrown in the ground, leaving them with cracks and scratches.

When people steal, they do it to gain what they need to survive and what they want to get.

Beware, because when they do it so much, they start feeling entitled to it. Suddenly, there is no way out. They keep stealing and will never stop.

Everything, including small areas which you'd never thought someone would open, were such a mess. The fridge, stained with bright crimson-red bloody handprints. And under it, drops of blood dripping down the fridge, onto the floor.

Most of it had already dried out. It had stained the kitchen drawers and had clearly been there for days with how dark and brown it had gotten.

The more I wandered and browsed the area, the more I lost hope in finding new evidence.

Though the fingerprints looked oddly familiar, they were almost impossible to gather any information from. They had been smudged, smeared and had been messed up.

Suddenly, a buzzing sound cut through the air and continued as everyone jolted and began to exchange confused looks, trying to figure out where the noise was coming from.

It didn't take long for us to realize the thrumming noise was coming from Charlotte's body.

I grimaced.

When I finally regained my senses and could finally lift my legs up and start moving, I carefully approached her, almost tip-toeing towards her body, not knowing what to expect when I got closer to her.

I hesitantly slipped a hand inside of her pocket and found the vibrating phone.

All of our hearts sank as I took the phone out of her pocket. I checked over the screen and eyed the unknown caller icon on the phone. I slowly placed my finger on the answer button before I started speaking.

"Hello? Who is this?" I questioned anxiously, unsure about what was about to happen. I had to press my lips together to prevent them from quivering.

There was no reply.

That was until what seemed like an audio recording glitching as it played.

A gut-dropping sound blared through the phone. It was what sounded like an injured man, fighting for his life. His last few words and final moments before he dropped dead. The person who attacked him had an unfamiliar voice, a voice that was almost not human-like.

His voice was hoarse, and he was audibly gasping for air as it seemed like he was being held down by something so strong, with no oxygen available.

They had been restricted to all movement to possibly save themselves and were slowly suffocating.

No matter how much the man seemed to twist or kick off from the ground, from the sound of him attempting to defend himself, he didn't budge from whoever was holding him.

We knew it was too late once the audio had gone completely silent.

That's when the audio recording had paused and stopped playing after they had hung up the phone.

We all stood still, filled with nothing but fret and an overwhelming feeling of discomfort. I had sweat dripping down the side of my head.

I quickly wiped it off with the back of my hand and glanced around worriedly, but no one seemed to have noticed.

I stammered as I muttered the only words I could get myself to say, "Guys, I need you to get working on tracking down everyone who has ever touched, seen or even been near this phone. We need to find out where this call came from."

Marcus jumped up from behind me and quickly replied, "On it. I need you to go take a break and then make sure to examine the crime scene one last time."

I forced a reassuring smile towards Marcus.

Even though I almost fell on my way because of my blurry vision, I staggered towards the bathroom and halted in front of the mirror.

Salty droplets beaded on my forehead and rolled down my temples, dripping onto the sink. I let out a labored, shuddering breath in an attempt to calm myself down.

As I stared in the mirror, a hint of red caught my eye. The color jolted me out of my headspace and that's when I noticed smeared blood droplets all over the bathroom. Covering the sink, the mirror, the toilet and every other possible area you'd never expect to find blood on.

I rushed out of the bathroom and called out for Marcus desperately. However, my voice fell on deaf ears and I came to the horrible realization that Marcus had left.

I buried my hand into my deep-stuffed pocket and jerked my phone free, ready to call Marcus. I quickly typed his number and shot my finger at the call button.

Marcus soon picked up.

"Hey, what's up?"

Marcus questions, confused.

I took a deep breath and swallowed the lump that was in my throat. It felt like my tongue almost went down with the saliva.

I started to explain, "There's blood everywhere, and I doubt it's Charlotte's blood. This could lead us straight to the murderer."

I patiently stood quietly, waiting for Marcus to respond to what I had just told him.

Eventually, five seconds turned into fifteen and that's when I finally took my phone off my sweaty ear, and noticed that *my phone had died* before I could even get a chance to tell him anything.

I remain statue-like for what felt like ages, not knowing what I would've expected Marcus to do if he were to hear what had happened.

I approached the bathroom one more time, but this time with my camera, ready to snap photographs of every little spot. I examined it carefully, making sure not to miss any details.

As I glanced at it longer, I noticed that the spots of blood were bright and looked fresh.

Looking down on the floor, I spotted syringes that were once loaded with an addictive potent drug. This murderer had been self-medicating after killing Charlotte.

I finally realized that the drops of blood belonged to the murderer after they accidently poked their skin when they tried to use one of the scientific equipment.

Who could these belong to? Who would want to murder her? I had to wait for the results to come back, which would sometimes take days.

I sprinted away from the bathroom, making sure to waste no time. I wanted to leave the crime scene as quickly as possible, while also making sure I did my job the way I was supposed to.

I made my way to the place where Charlotte's body was found, cold and bare.

Putting my bright-blue gloves on, I reached to unzip my bag that I had put on the table earlier that day. I took out my adhesive powder and delicately began to place it where I could pick out the smears of fingerprints.

Though they were smeared, there is no telling what lies beneath those prints, whether it be worthy of my time or not.

I then proceeded to get out the lifting tape, almost getting it stuck between the zippers of my bag, and readied to get as many of the fingerprints as I possibly could.

The more evidence I could provide, the better and easier it was to catch the murderer.

Once again, I reached out for my bag and then swabbed the dry blood. This will help us to find out who this blood belonged to.

I needed to find anything that would help to at least catch the murderer and lock them behind bars for a long time to come.

I had to make sure the doors behind those who commit crimes were sealed and never opened again. Though prison can be a thing that protects society from those who have done harm in their life, and have the ability to do it again, it may also be cold-hearted and indifferent for those imprisoned wrongfully.

For those people, it is an abusive building kept in place by fear systems that starve and abuse those populations and societies being forced to stay there. That is when it becomes cruel.

I've fallen victim to being wrongfully locked up behind bars. Around two years ago, my life had been flipped.

I went from being the most trusted person in my team to being the person no one could count on anymore.

What landed me in jail was something I never expected.

While I was driving around, I spotted a dead body on the sidewalk, and with there being no witnesses, I was the most obvious suspect. Originally, my sentence was five years, however, it got reduced to one.

These moments in life will never leave you. They will always be with you and taunt you for the rest of your life.

I remember waking up in prison every day, hoping and praying it wouldn't be the day I would be killed by one of the other inmates.

Even though being a detective sounds like it's an easy job, it's not. It takes almost all of your effort and it takes a lot of your time.

Even when you're not at work, you can't help but still work on cases in your free time.

There is no escape from it. Once you have entered the world in which I live, you will get so used to it, you won't think about anything else.

While working on Charlotte's case, I had to examine the whole crime scene, making sure not to miss anything.

Who knows, perhaps a tiny strand of hair will lead me straight to the murderer. Once I was examining it, I put anything and everything I could find into small plastic bags and handed it to the detectives standing beside me to examine it even further.

"And now we wait," I silently mumbled.

Though I knew I had to keep working on this case, I couldn't help but sneak a glance at the clock. It was about to strike midnight to my dismay, but that could account for why I felt so exhausted.

I sighed before getting my keys, preparing to make my way home.

During the drive home, all I could think about was how heavy my eyes felt. Thankfully, I managed to make it home in time without falling asleep on the wheel.

Chapter 3
Who Did It?

During the pitch-black night, graced and blessed with the ever-present stars and moon, I was jolted awake by the piercing shriek of sirens calling out from the river of traffic. I was shaken by the shrill sound of alarms blaring seemingly right outside and the repetitive flashing of blue and red lights shining through my window.

I leaned in from my spot on my bed to take a glance outside my window, and peered out to see the road flooding with police cars. Their dazzling red and blue lights were like a sore thumb against the night as they swarmed along the street.

Shocked by this scene, I threw myself into a sitting position and snapped my gaze to the bedside table. My clock sat there innocently, blinking in bright green numbers to read '3:37 AM'.

I turned my blank glare onto the nothingness present on my walls and embraced the most inviting of invitations, resting.

I couldn't bear the fact that I had yet another night with only a couple hours of sleep, but I soon realized that even if my body needed rest, my mind was desperate to move.

Despite this, my body was still sluggish and that feeling weighed me down until my back was on my mattress again. I began to doze again, but a string of harsh knocks pounded against my door with a noise similar to a clap of thunder.

The noise had startled me and snapped me back up. I stumbled off my bed, barely landing on my feet as I scrambled to get to my door.

I halted in front of the door, with alarms blaring at the back of my head and my heartbeat in my ears. I reached out almost hesitantly and placed my hand on the doorknob before slowly turning it.

The door creaked open, and revealed a blue uniform waiting for me on the other side. The police officer glared at me with a stern face that was filled with an unknown emotion, filled with nothing but seriousness. Her body was tense, and her shoulders were hunched as if she was ready to grab her gun and shoot me from where I stood.

I was barely able to keep my eyes open, but I managed to mumble something,

"Hey, is there something wrong?"

"Yes, actually. We have just found a dead body recently murdered and we need to question everyone who lives around here," she snapped with anger.

The volume of her tone snapped me awake, like drums being hit on both sides of my head.

"Wait, what? Is that why there were so many ambulances out there? I don't know anything. I just wo—"

I pleaded to her, before she started to cut me off.

"Listen, I'm not here to argue. Just answer and it'll all be okay. We just need to be thorough and make sure we have gone through everyone who may have had the chance to kill her," she stated with a clipped tone and a sneer.

I snapped back at her,

"Just stop, please. I've been running on three hours of sleep for the longest time. This day being one of them. Just please, stop questioning me and start questioning those who may have a motive. I've just been sleeping, I haven't been out."

I stood there for a long time, waiting for her to say anything else.

Finally, she began rolling her eyes, before she began talking, "That's what they all say. You've just been awake while there's sirens going off?"

I put all my frustration and anger into slamming the door behind me with a bang. The force of the door banging closed caused the walls to quiver and the picture frames on the wall to rattle.

I couldn't help but feel my knees trembling with weakness and leaning on the wall for support.

After a while of leaning on the wall, I carefully dragged my feet towards my bedroom to go back to sleep for at least a couple more hours.

I sat down on my bedroom floor and remained there to rest and gawked at the alarm clock. This time, I realized I had spent 30 minutes of my time sitting down on the icy, bare floor staring and thinking about what had just happened.

"What is going on out there?"

I whispered to myself, approaching the window to glance out of it one last time.

I could see the police officers questioning everyone on the streets before letting them go until eventually, the unwelcoming streets were deserted, with the exception of the police officers, left taking notes and examining the crime scene.

Even though I knew I lived in an area that was no stranger to crime, any time someone was murdered in my area, there was an overwhelming feeling of shock that would creep up on me.

Crimes would happen here almost every day, and the fact that I had spent my youth studying all about it would prepare me for dealing with the afterlife of those among me but I was wrong. No number of years will prepare people for the shock they'll face once someone they have met dies.

The fact that one person could go from being described as 'full of life' and the next second, people describe how good they were to everyone, all the good memories they made together and how much they would forever be missed.

Instead of returning back to my bed, I snatched my phone from its charger and darted to my coat rack to wear the first one I saw. I slipped into it before spinning on my heels and rushing towards my front door. I had to prepare and make a warm sanctuary in my own body to go outside in the cold weather.

I burst out of my house and slipped a hand into my pocket for my cell phone.

I was shaking from the cold weather as I fumbled with my phone, trying to scroll through my contacts list before my thumb landed on Marcus's number. I shot him a call and stopped in the middle of the sidewalk, waiting for him to pick up.

"Huh, hey? Why are you calling me? I'm so confused."
Marcus muttered in a tired and exasperated voice.

"Marcus, good. Listen, I just woke up to the sound of blaring alarms and I think we have a case. There's a dead body and the police are interviewing people," I replied, marveling at the good news.

I paused since I couldn't hear anything coming from Marcus' end.

"Marcus, you there?" I questioned, waiting for Marcus to say anything.

I could hear him swallow thickly before he replied, "Noah. Please just wait until morning. We don't need to discuss it right now."

"Wait, Marcus, please. Some other place will beat us and get this case before us."

I exclaim as I quickly try to convince Marcus to listen.

However, that wasn't enough to convince him otherwise. As I removed my phone from my ear, I could see that he had hung up before I could finish explaining and could tell that he didn't even bother to think about it. I inhaled sharply, taking in the cold wind in an effort to wake myself up more.

I crept towards the officer that I had previously spoken with in my apartment.

I try to utter the only words my mind could think of at the time, "Hey, uh. I've told you this already but I'm wondering if we could help you with your case. I'm a detective and I think the place I work might be able to help you."

The officer turned to look at me for a long moment before she crossed her arms and replied haughtily, "Just contact our head officer, I have no say in this. And, seriously? Is this really the time for you to ask me this? There's a dead body here."

She then looked away to peer down at her notepad, beginning to scribble something down but never once looking back up at me.

After a second, I slowly turned away to trudge back home while stuffing my hands inside my jacket's pockets to keep them warm.

I had given up for today. Just as I began to cross the road, cold splatters began to fall on my skin. I stopped and turned my gaze to the sky, blinking back my grogginess so that I could pick out the dark clouds against the even darker sky as the rain picked up.

It was like a blessing in disguise. I stood still, in the middle of the deserted road, looking up as my mind began to drift into peaceful emptiness.

I admired the glint of the rain droplets falling from above and the coldness that came with it. I breathed it all in and the only words to describe it would be a journey. The start of one that would lead down to hell.

In one moment, I was embracing the sudden weather in all its beauty as I stood on the road, and the next, a thundering bang shook me out of my trance. The acrid stench of oil and rubber burning cut across the air as the two mangled cars sat just yards away from me.

All the police officers ran to circle the cars, yelling at me to get out of the way and to leave.

I remained motionless for what felt like ages. For a moment, my brain felt like it was stuttering. My eyes felt like they were taking more light than they should be taking in and the ringing in my ears disoriented me. I managed to pick my feet up and start making my way back home.

I passed through the wave of smoke blowing away from the demolished cars. I couldn't do anything but cough and gag at the putrid stench.

It didn't take long for me to make it back after that. My throat and my lungs burned while my eyes felt dry. When I made it through my front door, I kicked off my shoes, hung up my coat, and went straight to bed.

Even as I laid on my bed, all I could do was stare at the empty ceiling of my bedroom while enjoying the warmth of my covers.

I couldn't bear to move, yet at the same time, all I wanted to do was stare outside and listen to the wailing sirens.

My head shifted on my pillow, and I looked over to the window. I stared at it for what felt like hours before I saw the ambulance speed away. I stared until the blaring sirens that had once called out to the night fade away into nothingness.

With night's silence back, I managed to relax and close my eyes to try and make the most out of the few hours I had left until I had to be awake.

Late at night in the city, with a stretch and a yawn, I settled myself into my duvet and leisurely managed to fall asleep.

I woke up suddenly.

Yet surprisingly it wasn't because of a noise or interruption, but just because my dream had ended. I took in the rays of sunlight slipping through my window, coming to the realization that I had definitely overslept. I confirmed this by glancing at the clock. Shining brightly in green, the time flashed 9:36 AM.

Usually, I wake up at around seven and earlier. It was relaxing to have enough sleep every once in a while. Yet, that came at the expense of me being behind on my work.

I picked up my phone from the nightstand and saw that Marcus had sent me messages about new suspects he found that we needed to interview.

I quickly got up from my bed and hurried into the shower. Being beneath the shower head, the water came soothing and warm. All I could think about was the text I had gotten from Marcus.

How many suspects were there to interview? Did one of them do it, or were we just wasting our time with them?

I left the shower, making sure to wrap myself in my towel and heading back to my room. I picked up wrinkled clothing from the floor and quickly slipped into them before grabbing everything that I knew I would need and ***attempted*** to rush out of the door.

Yet suddenly, my brain began to fog up and any thoughts I had went nowhere at all.

Memories came at me almost attempting to drown me.

One of them being:

"Do it–" I began exclaiming.

Yet Alice had already begun. Her ache was always so subtle; she sought solace in herself at all times. The moon had been witness to the weight of her emotions and how she got rid of all the pain that clouded her thoughts constantly with trembling hands.

"–or don't," I muttered slowly.

I was greeted with a loud bang following with silence.

Terror etched across my face, I burst through the door. At this point, my heart was up to my throat. As I entered, an immediate discomfort settled upon me. The chilling stillness and quietness was something you couldn't escape from. Looking around the bathroom, in search of answers, the haunting sight of someone I once knew was being portrayed in front of me.

Looking at the reflection in the mirror, I felt an ache in my heart. The haunting realization stung me; the person who I was staring back at was nothing more than a stranger. My eyes were empty.

Maybe there isn't as much silence as I thought, as I flung myself onto the floor: each one of my heartbeats echoing louder than the last. My chest tightened and taking each breath became a struggle. Inside, a voracious flame lit, the weight of it eating at me. The gnawing discomfort of guilt was taking a piece of my soul apart more and more. Leaving my tortured soul to attempt to go through with this, I felt the heavy burden of remorse slowly press upon me, making sure I was in pain. Suffocating the last vestiges of hope that flickered within my heavy heart.

Alice was dead.

I tried reaching for the door knob to leave yet I realized I couldn't. A nauseating feeling of hypocrisy sprung onto me. I had realized that my whole life was now doomed.

Droplets of sweat began rolling down my forehead while I was attempting to keep my heavy breathing steady.

Flashbacks upon flashbacks hit me.

Voices echoed through my mind, "Noah– stop plea–"

I slit her throat. I watched as the blood sprayed from her neck and rolled off; the act which stained the walls and furniture in her house. I could feel the resistance of her flesh and bones as I began cutting through. I gripped the knife tightly in my hand and saw her jerk her head back as she gasped for some air. The sound was sickeningly loud. Eventually, I heard the sound of the blood mixing with the air escaping her lungs. A gurgling death rattle. Her blood soaked the rug and seeped through the floorboards.

My lack of oxygen rendered me upon the floor as if I was being pushed and held down by a heavy weight, standing on my chest.

I quickly sat up and reached for my shoes and flung them off of me. I crept towards the kitchen and reached for the pain-killers over my counter to numb the pain I was feeling.

To wipe out the trauma I was experiencing.

The amount of lies I had told to myself and to everyone had an invisible barrier and there was no way to fight such a thing. ***There was no way to escape such a thing.***

My memory had blocked everything away, including all the revenge I had sought.

I've had enough people blaming me for things that were never truly my fault. All I heard every day in my life were:

Constant pleas, quiet yet so persistent, that always called for me to be one step forward and help everybody else.

No matter how grand or subtle the help people needed was, they always relied on me. Who was going to help me? All I wanted was for people to not depend on me.

The weight of responsibility would constantly press heavily on my shoulders and the very thought of just stumbling, of not living up to other people's expectations, felt like letting down not only myself, but all those hearts who looked up to me.

I'd had enough of the world casting hopeful eyes upon me, and yearning for me to rise and shoulder their burdens.

I had always had a constant fear, roaming around inside of me, yet it never seemed to go and leave me alone. How come it's me that has to be driven to overcome my own doubts and hesitations, for the sake of everyone else who placed their trust within me? I was desperate for a way out.

The world has always sought and pleaded for me to play the hero in this story, yet what if there was a villain inside all of us?

There is no if, rather we must learn to accept the truth. I'd go back and I'd do it all again if it meant the missing who deserve to be sought and found got justice.

We are all villains in other people's lives and through people's eyes.

All I am doing is changing that narrative. Perhaps one backstory, one sob story, can change someone's mind.

People say,

"It only takes one bad apple to spoil the bunch."

It keeps me wondering, what if I was the bad apple? What if there was no place here for me on Earth?

All it takes is one touch for the rest to spoil. What if the only place I belong is where all the rotten ones go?

The knife I had once used to carve out the bread into generous slices had been used to stab someone's kidneys and lead them to pain so great, they had no energy left to scream.

In the depths of my psyche, a chilling void and detachment from the realm of empathy took all hold of me.

The very thought of plunging a blade into those innocent individuals.

The very sensation of the blade slicing through skin and muscle is an eerie thrill that casts a sinister hue over me.

A cold fascination.

The cries of my victims reverberate like distant echoes, lost in the abyss of my very own emptiness. Their anguished cries and pleading gazes. Hell, I even framed Isabella's boyfriend for her own death.

Each victim is a prop in my performance. Their bodies are worth nothing more than for me to use for a dance of manipulation. Only for me to be able to test the limits of human vulnerability.

Their metallic tang of blood mingles with the acrid scent of fear, a perfect concoction that feeds the insatiable hunger for chaos that lives in the core of my being.

I felt nothing if not the opposite of remorse and guilt.

The only thing I felt was a twisted feeling of control over all of the victims that I had before their last moments.

Oh, how they thought they'd be able to convince me to let them go, but empathy is a foreign language to me, drowned by their desperate screams.

The more I kept thinking, the more the memories came upon me. Charlotte wasn't the only one I had murdered.

I had a habit of killing people whenever anything went wrong in my life. I had killed my best friend and people I didn't know.

All of them had a brutal ending.

Now, I would soon be found out for all the sins I had committed against people.

This book gave me one more adventure.

One last thing that I have spent all my years accomplishing; for every breath I spent searching for answers was half of the number of cries I had.

This is and forever will be my destiny.

Every murder is and forever will be the end of a story, but for others, they think of it as just the beginning of a new one.

As someone once said, "Life is worth so much more than gold, neither can be bought or sold."

Forever is infinite, yet not quite for us as life will come to an end, just like it did for me. For some people, forever isn't very long at all, while for others, they spend time waiting ages for people.

There are so many emotions in this world yet so little words and sounds that can explain those emotions – and with that, the pen I have used to carve writings into these pages is running dry.

"I'll find him, just you wait," I whispered, with my voice full of sorrow. I put down the maroon-soaked towel and accepted who I had become, or perhaps what I had become.

As the wailing sirens of the police cars pierced through my windows and came closer to my house, their announcement being clear, the air of the room grew heavy with tension.

The arrival of the inevitable was here. Blue and red lights began dancing across my walls as they had started making their entry. Time seemed to slow as their presence made me come to the realization.

The realization that the facade of secrecy had shattered. It wasn't only me who knew my secret.

My heart starts pounding in the rhythm of a drumbeat.

After many desperate attempts of trying to catch the murderer, it had all finally clicked and I came to the horrible realization that I had caught him.

I hadn't caught him today. I had unknowingly caught him a long time ago.

I had caught me,
I was the murderer.

THE END

Afterword

Recovered, multiple of Noah's poems were found.
I don't like looking up.
Perhaps the sky makes me feel too giddy.
As the raindrops greet Earth–
Most people adorn them.
They stand by watching as the priceless, crystal-clear
gemstones are almost like a present to those observant eyes.
The raindrops themselves–

    I trust more than anything.
Though raindrops aren't meant to last,
And were always meant to condense away from us humans.

    If it were at all possible,

    where rain would go, I would decide to go too.
To the point where carefully,

    the raindrops would start to spill the secrets I had
trusted them with,

    taunting and mocking me with them all.
Wherever I turned,

    /Pitter-patter/

/Pitter-patter/

    /Pitter-patter/

/Pitter-patter/

A never-ending cycle that I quickly realized will continue to torment me for the rest of my life–
    I eventually realized there was no escape from the mistake that I had helplessly made.

There the rain was–
    holding you accountable for the errors you made
when you were at your most vulnerable.
Those errors that those demonizing raindrops had slowly
convinced us to make.
Moonlight bleeds through the curtains,
    like adrenaline through my blood.
The moon bears witness to my unholy spree,
    my badge being nothing but a facade,
        concealing the stain I have bestowed upon
    the city.
There is greed deep beneath all of us–
    It may not always show.
    (But when it does.)
It spills secrets you never even knew you had.
Locked in there just as paint carelessly falls:

    /Split-splat/

/Split-splat/
    /Split-splat/

Your greed calls out for help.
    It screeches just like an animal that you'd expect it
to do nothing but bite and claw you onto the wall.

There you are once again:

   being labeled as a "monster."

And once more, there it all goes.

Everything we have ever worked for is quickly racing down
the drain.

However, once Earth figures out these secrets are
somewhere where they don't belong,

it quietly buries it deep where no one will disturb its peace.

   You may blame yourself for your greed–

   but the truth is, that it haunts everyone.

Evil and good.

Your greed is a sword in your guts–

   The only hand that can control it is yours.

What you decide to do is no one's choice but your own,–

   be kind, help others,

   and rest dear one.

You are the only rock and shelter you may seek

   you are the only rescue you may confide in.

No one other than you can control your actions.

   No one other than you can remove what you have
inflicted upon your soul.

If you so wish, you may be helped

   you may even decide to do the helping–

a death for a life,

   an old soul for a new soul

whatever you decide to do,

   make sure it has some sort of purpose.

In a fire of shame and guilt,

   there lies the ashes of your birth.

And some may think, it may just be one never-ending
sequence of life.

There is no life without one another,
without that one leaf or cloud–
        that one beetle or bird,
may just be the reason why you are here on Earth with us.
If every single one of us
        decide to feel to the core of our souls,
we may eventually start to realize,
        we may eventually start to understand,
that life is sacred.
Soon, we may all start to understand that life is the holiest of
gifts you may ever receive.
It is surely the most sacred of gifts that heaven can bestow
and present to you.
The only art I have ever been able to create
was painting the night with tones of despair.
A canvas of horror–
        Silent screams.
My victims' desperations echo
through my masterpiece.
I can't help but crave it more.
As their life ebbs away,
        with their final moments fast approaching.
Their very final breath escapes–
        and their soul is finally released from its cage.
        What is it that they'll miss doing most?
The world around us will carry on,
        just like it always has,
                and just like it always will.
The only difference now is,
one more body has departed from this mortal coil,
to perhaps another realm.

Their perishable body still lay–
Only this time,
it can't feel the warmth of the sun,
nor can it hear the beautiful melodies of life.
"I am not a monster,"
I try muttering out.
Yet, there lay an empty void in my heart,
not trying to find my journey of redemption,
not a slight flicker of remorse.
"I am not a monster,"
I repeat once more.
In the silent corridors of my weary soul–
Everyone looked at me.
Their reliance upon me became too heavy.
"I am strong,"
I whispered, trying to convince myself.
The weight was too much to handle
but what was I if not the most intelligent one of
them all?
"I am capable,"
I reassure myself,
barely being able to utter each word.
The weight of the world was too much to handle.
You may give me a glass–
And tell me to hold onto it,
to not let it slip.
What happens if my hand suddenly lets go?
What if the pressure for something so little
had gotten too much.
What if it had been a cold glass,
and I was the hot water.

What if the glass breaks?
Wails and anger seeping through its pores.
        With cries of agony.
Will they be disappointed by how poorly,
I kept the glass from breaking.
        Will I no longer be perfect?
My sanity would blur,
        I would start breaking.
        For when the world leans too much on my soul,
        bit by bit I start going away.
The darkness never went away.
It leaked through my body,
and caused nothing but sinister truth,
to be undone.
I yearn for pain,
I yearn to confront the abyss I have made–
To bleed in the darkness,
        and perhaps feel the essence of life.
I yearn for the string of reality–
words to so slowly pierce my soul,
betrayal's shards to carve my bitter life
and for agony to envelope me.
I will never again fall victim–
        to the deceptiveness of sweet deceit.
        Oh, how much I regret,
        falling in love with hope.
Its thorns were meant to protect me,
        not stab
and pierce me at every chance it got.
A numbness resides,
        in the depths of my soul.

In this abyss,
       a veil of darkness,
       a sense of dread,
suffocates me.
For in love's sweet grasp,
       I gave it my all.
A desperate bargain–
       A soul betrayed.
In the depths of the darkness,
       A sinister exchange happened.
In the devil's grasp,
       the deal was sealed.
In the devil's grip,
       my essence was sold.
I had sold my soul,
       for a tiny ember I wasn't promised.
A glimmer of hope.
       Oh, had I just sold my soul for love?
       In Love's Redemption,
       I'll find my way.
       In love's rebirth,
       I'll be set free.
Was I too far gone–
       Was I still able to plead for mercy?
I mourn the loss of someone I've never met–
       Perhaps it's the loss of myself.
A part of me will forever ache,
       even if you have moved on.
You can force my palate,
       down my throat.

Maybe even pour it down,

      before making me swallow.

You can tie me to a textured tree–

      And leave me so you may be.

You may leave me to slow down my pulse,

      and tie my light tongue.

You can even drive us to the riverside,

      And tell me to sit still,

         by the rocks.

However,

don't be surprised if you just so happen

to find a body,

pockets overflowing with stacks of little pebbles.

Hands turned to ash,

      and the once rosy cheeks were now pallid,

      sunken beneath a mask of death.

Sometimes I wonder if this life is eternal damnation.

Will I die hating the reality I lived in?

I wish–

      To be able to fall asleep in a boat,

      swaying side by side,

in the middle of the ocean,

in the middle of a lake,

      or even in the middle of nowhere.

I want the water,

      to be a portal to heaven.

So serene,

      so peaceful.

I only wish,

for the eyes of the ocean,

to only have a tranquil gaze to it–

whenever I am around.
I want to wake up,
on that same boat,
and not be saved by anyone–
Nor do I want the water to sweep me away.
Only the eyes of you.
> Blue in all certainty that they love me
> And mine will mirror the message–
> Except the color will be tinted brown.
I was exhausted–
> I walk a realm where reality doesn't exist,
> where whenever I tread past a path,
> I hear whispered echoes from unseen lips.
My mind's theater,
> a cruel illusion catering to my mind.
My mind's kaleidoscope,
> a gallery of images twisted with lies.
I threw salt on slugs
and watched as their existence marred.
I watched as they helplessly withered in pain–
> And their tender bodies twisted.
> So cruel, so vile.
I watched as they turned to soil,
> poisoned and scarred.
Beneath my feet,
> lay a reflection of darkness.
I wrote my name in the soil's despair,
a signature left to haunt them.
I wrote my name in the soil's despair
as if I were dealing with their loss.
A mark to be the victim.

The shadow peaks
>and the wind begins to speak.
There,
>lay my silver-laced tears–
>Watering your decaying grave.
Yet all that grows,
>are the suffocating memories,
>of the embers we once called love.
I searched
and found the keeper of death wanting,
>Yet, they didn't accept me.
I beg Persephone to let me join you,
>in the eternal resting place.
But Persephone doesn't kill me.
How can you meet up with a soul,
>who hasn't crossed,
onto the star-flung land,
they call death.
I will bury my hand–
>Through the venom-filled sands,
>with scorpions crawling through.
To see if I will get stung.
>Yet every day,
Their black eyes make my pulse stop.
I want to leave,
>but the scorpions will follow me.
I want to be left alone,
>but wherever I am,
>they too are.
The toxin will begin to build
and I will be filled with venom.

The poison will spread through my veins.
> Until I am a weary nothing.
> I can't help but plead,
> just to wait for them to leave me be.
Wrap a piece of string–
> Around my dull heart.
I'll wince in pain,
> as it punctures my veins
Let the blood drip onto the,
> blank canvas.
Just as paint would.
> Allow the piece of string,
> to guide you along the canvas.
And let it write letter upon letter–
> Draw for you hearts upon hearts.
A deep crimson color–
> That casts a naze each time sunlight hits.
of everything my empty heart could never say to you,
> yet it had always intended to.
Splashes–
> of your fragments,
resemble the feeling of:
> Sharp, splintered wood.
With each spray,
Moments of joy slowly rewind.
I quickly notice,
> there isn't much there.
Just small snippets.
Yet,
how come these memories are left there,
> etched within our souls,

unable to find a way out.
Tears slip away,
>	crashing down like fragile glass beads.
Here I lay,
>	in this room of solitude.
And,
It seems like I am the only one remaining.
Everyone else has moved on,
>	and left the memories where they belong,
back into Earth's loneliest place,
>	stashed away from everyone.
>	*Isolated.*
I was too scared–
>	To love the sun,
with all it's warm rays,
acting like an ignited fire,
>	towards us all.
Yet,
>	everyday,
when the sun set,
>	I was fearing the future.
What if tomorrow will be the day the sun never rises again.
So I close my eyes,
>	and bury myself in sand.
And stayed there because of how worried I was.
By the time I got out,
>	The sun had set again.
I had never actually managed to enjoy the sun–
>	*until perhaps it was too late.*
The strongest emotion I have ever known how to express
was anger.

Art is expression,

And my medium of choice was painting.

Each stroke was a release,

I longed and sang of chaos.

The walls around me were red;

       A deep color that would cast a haze throughout the

home

       whenever the sunlight hits.

It became a scorching canvas,

mirroring my soul with the intense heat of unspoken words,

and smoldering emotions.

And no modern notion of retaining the both of us–

       Could ever permeate the atmosphere.

Except through antiquated souls and pretending godful but

truly godless fools.

It's difficult to become the devil when you were never an

angel.

And oh, I'll be damned–

if I permit the devil to murmur to you,

sinister ideas and simmering passions.

A dance with demons,

where the darkness dwells.

Should I wait for the artist to better himself,

       for the crimson to blur away?

Should I wait for the artist to better himself,

       or rather should I find another fool to work on?

The fool was never really a fool

but craved the feeling of being sculpted.

What if the artist could become the art–

       no one has ever noticed my desire to

       become someone's muse.

The aspiration of the listener,
        to be listened to.
        Perhaps I was born to create art
        and never become it.
I suppose I will never live eternally,
in the pages of someone's book.
        To be held tenderly in ink.
If only I–
        Could be turned into stone,
        during any given moment.
Oh, how much power
I'd be able to hold over humanity.
It'd make the devil, so jealous,
maybe even feel weak.
And perhaps it'll make him forge his acceptance.
        And make him repent.
It would allow me to think–
        Maybe even for years at a time,
        for thoughts that require a couple of minutes at
most.
It would allow,
        for me to cater to the minds of humanity,
and help them find something they need.
Something so unholy,
that their minds had been so wrapped around,
with the facade of goodness,
that they never found out what they truly wanted.
Oh–
The trickster devil, he can't be beat.
Beneath his mask
        of friendly guise,

lurks in darkness.
A web chain of lies.
Oh–
The trickster devil, playing his part.
He speaks no kind words towards you–
Only poison-like words,
holding daggers and leaving his mark on you.
His intentions unseen,
yet perfectly clear.
Oh, how can I stay safe?
From the trickster devil,
and his wicked craving.
In the ocean's vast expanse,
Your paintings are too similar to mine,
for us to not be the same.
Please, tell me,
Are you from the past?
Are you from the future,
coming to warn me of my destiny?
Perhaps we are nothing more
than living memories.
All I ask from you,
is to tell me.
Tell me which way the wind is blowing–
So that I know where to turn.
Tell me which way the wind is blowing–
So that my eyes and hair no longer touch.
Just tell me one thing,
Where are you now?
I want to reminisce,
perhaps even dream.

Please just tell me.
		Tell me what it feels like to have lived.
Intricate prints–
		Embedded into a sphere of complexity.
It's whole existence enduring mental misery.
No two humans are alike.
So how can you possibly fathom me?
Disquieted emotions fill my head–
		For every day you spend,
		trying to get the world to understand you,
you'll drive yourself insane.
		You exist in your world,
		while others are simply being.
So tell me, how can you possibly fathom me?
Carry the lessons of your trauma.
No one else can fathom you,
		don't try to get them to.
I tried my best to put a name to the face
And a voice to the lip's movements
Discovered my auditory senses failed me,
		and attempted mental contortions,
		only to realize clear vision was all I required.
Persuaded myself that even if my name remains unspoken,
you still recognize who I am.
Convinced myself that you will eventually attach a name to
the face,
fabricated a narrative for the sake of illusory contentment.
I don't want to stand at the door anymore.
I must live a life of duty,
because it's the only way I'll be satisfied.
I'll live less like myself,

and more like what people want me to be.
I am a willing servant.
I will live a life of duty.
Life had won once again.

Let me in, please,
I promise I'll be good.

"Think Of Me Once In A While, Take Care."